A STALKER'S OBSESSION

PEARL'S NARRATION

Made with ♥ on the Notion Press Platform
www.notionpress.com

The book is dedicated to all the daydreamers who are never going to give up on their dreams.

Contents

Foreword *vii*

Acknowledgements *ix*

Prologue *xi*

1. Prachi- My Weird Personality 1
2. Prachi- Dream Vacation 8
3. Prachi- The Inevitable 14
4. Prachi- Brewing Up A Storm 20
5. Arjun- The Chasing Begins 25
6. Prachi- Entering The Cage 29
7. Arjun- My Fucking Heart 33
8. Prachi- Pleading The Predator 37
9. Prachi- Guilty Conscience 44
10. Arjun- First Step To The Right 48
11. Prachi- The Fucking Emotions 53
12. Arjun- Agitation In Paradise 56
13. Prachi- Crumbling Walls 59
14. Arjun- Thawing A Stone 65
15. Prachi- Losing It 69
16. Arjun- Finally In My Arms 74
17. Prachi- On Fire 79
18. Prachi- Falling For Him 84
19. Arjun- Worth It! 89
20. Prachi- Changes With Anxiety 92
21. Arjun- Finding Peace 95

Contents

22. Arjun- So Pure And Naive! 99

23. Prachi- The Revelation 105

24. Arjun- Raging Heart 109

25. Prachi- Gratitude 112

26. Prachi- So Fucking Hot! 117

27. Arjun- The Temptress 120

28. Prachi- The Celebration 125

29. Prachi- Blast From The Past 129

30. Prachi- Fucking Frying Pan! 132

31. Arjun- Baffled 138

32. Arjun- Powerless 143

33. Prachi- Regenerated 147

34. Arjun- Walking Into The Fire 150

35. Prachi- Blissful 153

About The Author 157

Foreword

This book is a beautiful story that revolves around two successful individuals falling in complicated
love together while dealing with love and bereavement. Can be considered a pure mixture of
originality, beauty, fantasy twisty-turniness, and poignancy. If you are a fan of romance, fantasy, and
erotica novels, I would 100% recommend this book to you. Overall I thought the book was absolutely
brilliant as the background was epic, the description was inspiring, and the characterization was
practically flawless, covering just the right amount of sympathy, love, and hate at the same time.
- Pooja Yadav

Acknowledgements

I would like to express my immense gratitude to my parents who always stood behind me. Through every failure of my life, they were there standing like a wall to protect me. I would also like to say thanks and show my love for my dear husband who always makes me laugh doesn't matter how moody I become. I would like to show my respect and gratitude for my In-laws who are very supportive, loving, and caring.

I would like to say thank you and show my love for all my cousins. They are the only people in this world after my parents, who love me and accept me just the way I am.

Last but not least, I would like to say thank you to my editor, Pooja Yadav. Not only did she help me in enhancing this book but she has been an amazing cheerleader encouraging me and helping me throughout the process.

Thank you.

Prologue

"What do you want?" she seems curious.
"You," I wink at her.
"What do you mean by me?" her cheeks are red now. I chuckled. "Well, when I say 'you,' I mean
all of you. Everything of you. The choice is yours." I gave her a coy smile. The bread toast she
was chewing slides off her hand, and her mouth opens in a complete 'O'.
"You are the devil himself, aren't you? Or do you take private lessons from Lucifer himself?" her
cheeks are flushed.
"Well, you can say it is an inborn talent.", I say thoughtfully, scratching my beard.

1

Prachi- My weird personality

I'm shifting my position on the bed from side to side. By now, I should have gotten out of bed. I get up at five every morning to begin my day. But I find it challenging to do it every single day. It's not as if I'm a slacker or something. I try to avoid painful thoughts at all costs, but they only begin to enter my foolish head when I first wake up. But, after reading a book about getting up early and having a productive day, it lodged in my head like tentacles. I suppose the authors of such books didn't include information on how to avoid insomnia.

My business partner Ria and I run a content production and digital marketing company. Damn! That woman is brilliant. My life revolves around work and my parents for the last three years. To get to where I am now, I had to put in much effort, make a lot of sacrifices, and go through a lot of heartaches. Yet, I am grateful for all that has occurred in my life. I'm proud of myself for accomplishing this. There was a moment when I could not even contemplate realizing my dream. But, when Ria entered the picture, the rest became history. As time passed by, she became my best friend, and even then, we have been great friends. Together, we founded D&G Pvt. Ltd., which is now a brilliant success.

I want nothing more in life than to find someone who can cause my heart to race. Well, isn't that romantic and dreamy? But the hurt from the past is what really depresses me. Even if you offer someone your entire being, all you will ever experience is pain. I gave up on the notion of love and marriage for that reason. It makes no sense to waste energy there.

I couldn't be happier to live in my ideal home in Jabalpur with my parents. Now that I spend more time with her, my mother always has a smile on her face. Following my first achievement, I built this house. My father had a dream of owning a farmhouse. He had always imagined living this life. So, I created it for him. I cherish this home. In the villa's backyard, all the farming is being done. In front, there is a tiny lawn with a lovely pathway. My floor connects to an extra little penthouse with an external entrance. Ria now occupies the space. I also have a lovely library. It was always my wish to have my own library. I have always resembled Belle from "The Beauty and the Beast," the fairy tale. Having a book in my hand makes me feel a lot better than chatting with the petty people around. And for that very reason, I don't actually have many friends. Except for Ria, of course, with whom I get along well only because we are both nerds. Ria joins me in Jabalpur whenever I'm not in Bangalore. She is an orphan and doesn't have a family of her own, so I always make sure she comes along. She longs for a family atmosphere like my parents, who view her as their second daughter. Without her, I'm unsure how I would have gotten to where I am now.

Also, my floor has a great rooftop view of our agricultural area on the backside. I usually work out there. We've planted several trees, including mango, custard apple, pomegranate, and other varieties. Then we grow every vegetable. We have a tiny greenhouse in the center. We grow seasonal or temperature-sensitive fruits and vegetables. It is my sanctuary and feels good here.

Despite having all I could want in life, I often feel lonely these days. I wish I had someone I could just hang out with for a while. Someone who could energize me. I've experienced a good number of relationships. With heartbreaks, a void takes place in our hearts. Doesn't matter how much you try to fill it, it remains empty, I guess. Whenever someone tries to pursue me, the demons in my head push them away. They have established a permanent home there.

I get out of bed and immediately head to the bathroom to brush my teeth. I can see the emotionless eyes when I look in the mirror at my reflection, or at least that's what my mother thinks. No matter how much they love me, my parents won't be able to see how hollow I am on the inside. I then begin my daily meditation practice. Since a year ago, I have been meditating, and I'll be honest: I do it to keep myself calm. I struggle with anxiety and a short temper. My OCD is the most grating thing. I become annoyed whenever things don't go my way. But meditation has been a huge help to me. It doesn't make me any less irritated, but somehow I keep from getting angry and snapping at people. There was a time when I used to become angry at the slightest movement of any of my possessions.

I finish my meditation routine and then begin my martial arts exercise on the roof of my home. My father introduced me to it. He had concerns about a side of me that he had seen when I was a child. This is another habit I've developed to manage my stress. It takes a lot of energy to run a business, but I'm not complaining because it keeps me engaged most of the time. We have been attempting to close a contract with a London-based company for months. It's turning my and Ria's heads into fucking pudding.

After finishing my morning workout, I face the home directly in front of mine across the street. A house is being constructed there that is almost finished. That suggests that a new family will soon move there. In simple terms, I want some quiet neighbors. I hate nosy aunties and uncles who don't respect personal space. They appear to be wealthy based on the house's appearance, but who can tell? Money doesn't teach people manners anymore, does it?

In exactly an hour, Ria is going to chew my brain off. She is going to dump the entire day's schedule on me. She is such a blessing to have in my life. She has supported me every step of the way on my road to achievement. Along the way, she also blossomed. She is intelligent, knowledgeable, and loyal to her feet. When we first met, she had returned from college. She carried all the responsibility and allowed me to put down my thoughts on a blank sheet of paper. She is one of my favorite people and is quite adept at reading my emotions. She knows when to push and when to back down. She is one of the few people in my life who doesn't take my shits. But her bubbliness wears me down most of the time. She never shies away from being honest with me or giving me a reality check.

Every morning I take a long shower. I dressed in my formal wear. To remind myself of my plans for the day, I dress in a blouse and formal slacks. In the world of male-dominating vultures, it is crucial to be taken seriously as a female businesswoman.

Just as I'm about to head downstairs for breakfast after finishing, Ria enters the room. I give her a cold stare. She then asks, "Shall we get started?" while glaring at me with all her confidence. "Can I eat peacefully first?" I groan in response.

"You say it to me every morning, yet every day we end up discussing daily tasks. What's the point of waiting?" She gives me an eye roll.

She started talking incessantly about the course of the day, and I had to keep telling myself to relax and take in the moment. Even though I can handle all the work, I tend to "go with the flow" in most situations. After finishing my breakfast, I told my parents to enjoy themselves. From

Sunday through Wednesday, I'm in Jabalpur. I stay in Bangalore from Thursday to Saturday to conduct business and enjoy some alone time. I have my apartment in Bangalore. Spending a day or two per week alone helps me get myself together. Every Thursday, Ria and I take a flight to Bangalore to attend a weekly meeting at 10 a.m. And that's how my life continues.

PPP

I returned to Jabalpur early on Sunday to spend the day with my parents. I notice that the front house is a little crowded as soon as I arrive at my home. The neighbors have finally decided to move into their new home. I guess they are throwing a housewarming party.

When I enter my home, I find that my parents are getting ready to leave.

"Where are you both going?"

"We're going to the neighborhood housewarming celebration. We got the invitation yesterday. They asked us to attend the puja they would be having. So here we go." my mother replied.

I look at them as if I don't understand what they are saying, but I get my expressions together. They feel lonely at times with old age. So I don't ask any further and go to my office and start working.

My mother shows up and asks, "You want to come with us and meet our new neighbors?"

I look at her, "I have some work to finish. You go and have fun. "

Ria enters and asks, "What's happening outside?"

"Our new neighbors are having a housewarming party."

"Wow! And did they invite us? "

"Yeah, if you want to go, you can join my parents."

"Great! I want to see the inside of that enormous house. "

I roll my eyes and resume my work. After half an hour, I get a text from Ria saying, "You need to come here pronto."

I panicked, thinking something had happened to my parents, and I ran to the next door. I see people all in traditional attire, talking and laughing. I try to find Ria and my parents. I finally see my parents smiling and talking to a few people who look very nice and gentle by nature. I called Ria immediately, "Where are you?"

"I am near the swimming pool in the lawn area."

"What was so urgent that you called me here, Ria?"

"Just come here and you will know."

I try to find my way towards the lawn area and look for Ria. I find her standing with a guy, holding a cola drink and laughing like a fool. I reach her and ask, "What was so urgent that you called me in such a hurry?" "Look there." She points me to a guy, and I squint my eyes in the sunlight and freeze. What the hell? How did this happen?

Arjun walks toward me in a traditional kurta pajama, looking hot. He looks at me and smiles like he has seen the best person in the world. My heart races to the moon. I forgot how to breathe. This can't be happening.

"Hello Prachi, how are you?"

I lost the ability to talk clearly. Any word would have been appropriate. I instead turn around and run back to my house. I enter my office, close the door behind me, and begin to suffocate. It felt like I didn't breathe until I got to my room.

2

Prachi-Dream Vacation

I still can't believe he is here. I met Arjun almost a year ago in Goa. I went on a trip with Ria. We were working our asses off. And once we successfully completed five contracts back to back, Ria said we needed a vacation. Honestly, I needed it too. We both went, and I worked hard to get my mind off my ex-boyfriend. And going on vacation meant a lot of time for thinking about the unthinkable. So I decided, rather than thinking, I could go drinking. And from the point of starting the journey, I was drunk. I was feeling fantastic. I was enjoying the new money and the luxury. Thanks to the fancy hotel, classy drinks, and bitchy clothes, I was in a good mood. Ria and I decided to go to an open beach party on our third day. I was drunk and tired then, but I lived in the moment. I promised myself that I would enjoy every second of this trip.

We reached the party; it was evening time, and the beach was incredible. The cold air breezed through my hair, and I wore a cotton strappy white floral dress to my knee. Ria met a guy and was having a good time with him. I was holding my beer, sitting on the beach, and looking toward the sea, lost in my thoughts. At that moment, a guy comes and sits beside me and says, "Isn't it beautiful?"

I look at him, and my heart skips a beat. I have never seen a guy this hot and sexy in my life. Guys like him are usually on magazine covers or in movies. But not, in reality, sitting beside you, holding a beer and gazing at the sea. I replied," It is. No words can express the calmness it is

giving me right now."

He smiles at me in a sexy way, and I get jittery all over my body. He sips his beer and all of a sudden asks, "You want to come dance with me?"

I look at him with embarrassment on my face. "I am sorry, I am not good at dancing."

He laughs, "I can make you dance."

When he sees my hesitation, he pushes a little more, "Come on! Live a little. What's the worst that can happen?"

I look at him and think I want to live a little, and I nod at him. He takes my hand, and we move towards the group where people are dancing, and he starts grooving.

And in a few minutes, I am dancing with him. I guess he can make me do anything, and I won't say no at any point. I was living the life. We drank some more, and it was almost 10 at night after dancing for hours. We go to the beach and talk for hours. He keeps making me laugh. He is flawless. He reads because he likes to read. It's a first for me to meet a guy this hot. He is like his own kind of person, unique and smart. He also likes to play with words, which is fun for me. And then I realized it was already midnight. I finally stood up and said, "I think I should get going. It's late."

He stands and comes close to me and says, "I don't want you to go."

I froze for a minute. He comes closer to me, and I am only thinking about kissing his lips. He takes my hand in his, pulls me closer, and starts kissing me. That was the best kiss ever in my life. It was like finding water in a desert, quenching my thirst. He keeps kissing me for a very long time, and finally, when he stops, I start panting.

"I want to spend more time with you, so if you have to get going, then take me with you," he said. At that moment, I think it was my drunk brain that started processing everything. And I took his hand and started moving towards my hotel. We reach the hotel lobby, and I try to take the room key from my sling bag. He holds me from behind around my waist and starts kissing and sucking on my neck. I open my room with a lot of difficulty, and then he enters the room, and I stand outside.

I wondered what I was doing when Arjun looked at me with hungry eyes. And his gaze turns into tenderness. He comes closer, puts his hands on my waist, and says, "Don't overthink it. We can just sit and talk."

I hesitantly put a smile on my face and entered my room. I put my sling bag on the table and kissed him again. The kiss becomes very passionate, and we start to go at it. He picks me up, puts me on the bed, and starts kissing me on my jawline. And then he moves towards my neck and starts sucking. I turn into jelly all over my body. I start to moan, and his kiss becomes more rigorous. He pushes the straps of my dress aside and at a slow pace starts kissing my boobs over my bra. I am wearing a soft, see-through lace bra. He starts sucking my nipples over my bra, and I start clenching downward with wetness. He removes my dress along with my bra and goes around my waist. He starts sucking my belly button, and I start shaking. He goes straight south and kisses my inner thighs. "You smell amazing. What's your favorite smell?"

"Lavender and lemongrass," I whispered.

"You have the sexiest ass in the world."

"Ummm..." I forgot how to repeat words. He removes my white lace panties and starts licking and sucking on my clit. I started to convulse. It was the most fantastic head anyone ever gave me. I came onto his face in a few minutes. He made me come again and again until I started begging him to be inside me.

Finally, he removes his shirt and pants. I started appreciating his naked body. He was like a model with a V-shaped body and tanned abs. His ripped muscles made me wish I could lick them all night long.

"Like what you see, baby?"

"Baby, very likey." I started giggling. I was not able to believe that a guy like him was with me. He was in his boxers, and he came up to me and asked," What do you want to do, babe?"

"I want to lick you all over."

"Go for it.", he nudges his head at me.

I moved towards him, kissing his cheek and licking his nipple. He shudders in response. I lick and suckle his nipple more, and he groans, "You are hot."

I move towards his abs and lick each one of them. Then I reached for his boxers. I pull it down and gape in response. He is big and thick. I took him in my hand, started jerking, and put my mouth over his tip. His pre-cum started dripping, and I started sucking him deep. He groans and

moans while gripping my hair. He holds my head and starts fucking my mouth. I started to gag, and he came into my mouth after a few minutes.

He looks at me, "You are awesome."

He moves me to bed and starts kissing my lips with urgency tasting himself. He grabs my boobs and goes animalistic this time. He bites and pulls my nipples through his teeth, and I moan loudly, "Arjun."

"Yes, baby, keep screaming my name."

I forgot what was happening to me. He pushed his middle finger into my core and started finger fucking me. I felt like I was in heaven. Never have I ever had an experience so amazing. He kept me on edge and made me beg again and again to let me come. "Arjun, please, I need you inside me right now."

"I got you, baby."

And he gradually began to enter inside me, and I screamed in agony, "Shhh... baby relax. You must let me in."

It took me a while to get used to his size. I slowly started breathing, and then he started moving inside me. At some point, I gave up all the restraint that was inside me and started enjoying the moment. And then, he kept making me scream his name endlessly the whole night.

I spent the rest of my vacation days with him. I realized he was one of the most exciting people in the world. He has a weird personality, though. He talks and seems like an easy-going guy, but I felt he had a dominant side within him. I saw that side of him in bed very well. On my last day in Goa, he asked me when he would meet me again. And at that moment, my bubble of joy bursts into a million pieces. And I decided it was best, to be honest, and say, "I don't think we can meet again. I am in a very bad and busy place in my life right now. I took this vacation to feel better and you have been the main highlight of it. But I don't want to get involved right now."

"But what we have is great. I have never felt this way with anyone in my life. Do you think you can let it go?"

"I am sorry, but I have to. I know I am not being fair, but I don't want any distraction in my life right now." I see his face struck with hurt, and I turn away from him and go to my hotel room. I felt like my brain was going to explode, but I packed my bag and texted Ria, asking her to leave immediately. Because if I had stayed any longer, I would have gone weak.

3

Prachi- The inevitable

Present-day.

How can this happen? How can he be here? Ria comes to my room and shuts the door, "Why did you run like you saw a ghost?"

"What the hell is he doing here?"

"That is his house, you duffer!" she replies.

"Oh, God!" I groan.

"I thought you liked him a lot when you met him in Goa."

"Yeah, I liked him a lot and it was the best time of my life. But I don't want any complications in my life right now. My life is going so well."

She looks at me with a confused expression, "Why will your life become complicated because of him? Prachi just because your previous relationship was not good, doesn't mean this one will be the same as well. And you can be friends if you don't want anything but you can't run from him always if he is going to be your neighbor."

"We slept together for the whole time in Goa. I can't be just friends with him."

"I understand, but calm down. Don't think much about it.", She hugs me.

I look at her and nod.

The whole day kept thinking of Arjun. How is it possible that the man I met and had a casual time with ended up being my neighbor? He is damn sexy, and it's like he is a magnet pulling me towards him. I spent almost four days with him and never asked him his last name. Arjun Dixit! He is from Jabalpur as well. I mean, how can this much coincidence be possible?

I get frustrated by the end of the day and finally go down for dinner with my parents. My parents were talking about the housewarming party, how excellent everything was, and how nice our neighbors were. I listen to them quietly and eat my food. Ria keeps looking at me once in a while, and I avoid eye contact with her.

I hardly got any sleep last night. When my alarm buzzed, I returned to my routine and started my day as usual. And the whole day got by. I didn't get out of my house at all. In the evening, when I go to the living room, I find a woman almost my age sitting and chatting with Ria. I sit there while Ria introduces me to her, "Hey Prachi, this is Sameera. She is our neighbor and Arjun's younger sister. I met her yesterday at the housewarming party."

"Hello. How are you?" I greeted her politely.

"I am good. How are you?" she replies. She is gorgeous and petite.

"I am good as well. Are you liking this neighborhood?"

"Yeah, it is pretty peaceful. But I stay in Bangalore."

"Oh, that's great. We stay there as well for half of the week. What do you do?"

"I am a fashion designer. I have my boutique in Indiranagar. You should come sometime. I can design you a customized dress if you want for any particular event. You have an amazing figure and I would love to make you make my muse. I don't have many friends there."

I smile at her and say thanks.

"Where were you staying before and when did you move to Bangalore?" Ria asks.

"I was staying in Delhi with my parents after I graduated. I was doing a job in my brother's company but it didn't hold any interest to me. I always wanted to be a fashion designer. So I finally opened my store in Bangalore."

Impressive! It was very unlikely for a woman from a rich family to start from scratch in her life. "So you don't know anyone in Bangalore?" I ask.

"No, I only opened my store in Bangalore because my brothers are staying there."

"Oh!" That was all I could react to. So Arjun has one more brother.

"So, what do your brothers do?" Ria asks very casually. I look at her, giving her the eye.

Sameera replies, "They have construction and real estate business."

Great! He is in the real estate business. I keep quiet and let them talk. Ria finally makes plans for Friday night, and we agree to go for a drink in Bangalore. I go back to my office and resume my work.

ᑭᑭᑭ

On Thursday, we fly again to Bangalore for our morning meeting. And I get back to my work mode. Somehow, I finally got Arjun out of my mind. When Friday evening arrives, Ria reminds me of our plans with Sameera.

I finish my meetings and head back to my apartment to get ready. Honestly, I was looking forward to the evening. It had been a long time since I had a girl's night. I wear a black A-line dress with a silver wedge heel. I wash my hair and blow-dry it. Wear a good amount of make-up.

I like to doll up once in a while to look good. Ria comes to pick me up, and we reach the pub. We go inside and meet Sameera. She is beautiful even though she is short but has her sexiness.

They order some mocktails; I order bourbon for myself. We talked and started to have fun. I am starting to like Sameera a lot. She asks, "Shall we go to the dance floor?" And we all go to the dance floor and start grooving to the music. After some time, Sameera waves her hand to someone. When I look at who it is, I see Arjun and another guy waving back and coming toward us. The other guy must be his brother then. Arjun has a quirky smile on his face, and he is wearing faded jeans, a white t-shirt, and a jacket. He is looking dapper and damn sexy. I start feeling a warmth in my body as he moves towards me and says, "Hello Prachi. How are you? I hope you are not going to run again." My face flushes with embarrassment; I look at him and say, "I am good. And sorry for last time. I was just shocked. How are you?"

He smiles at me, "I am good as well. Would you guys mind if we join you in dancing?" We shake our heads and start dancing together. He introduces me to his brother Rahul, and I shake hands. Arjun comes closer to me and starts swaying the same way as in Goa. My whole body warms up with his closeness. I can't take my eyes off him the whole time, and his eyes are also on me. We danced for almost an hour. Finally, Ria says, "I am tired. Let's go and have some drinks. We get back to our table and order some starters and drinks. I ordered a double for myself. Arjun keeps looking at me throughout the evening, but we don't talk anymore. Around 11 PM, we decided to go home. Ria mentions that she wants to join Rahul in some other club.

Sameera is the youngest, and she joins them as well. Since Ria was my ride, I tried booking a cab for me. Arjun was standing near me; he snatched my mobile from my hand and said, "I'll drop you, come on." I looked at him, surprised, and said, "It's ok. I'll take a cab."

"Prachi, you don't have to act like we are strangers. We can be friends, right? Let me drop you. It's already late, and it's not safe."

I didn't know what to say. I didn't want to be like this as we would be meeting again and again. So I just said yes and gave my address.

Once we got in his car, I looked at him, "Have you told your brother and sister?"

"Prachi I was in Goa with my siblings."

"So they know about us?"

"Yes, and it is ok. They don't interfere or make any judgments in my life and I don't do the same for them."

"Please don't take it the wrong way, but I want to make it clear that I don't want my parents to know about us ever. Also, I don't want to start anything as well. I don't have any place in my life right now for anything other than my work and my parents. And whatever small

time I get, I like to spend it with friends like tonight."

"Hmm... Well, that's disappointing but I understand. I wanted to ask if I could take you out for dinner, but it's ok. You have made it clear. But can we be friends? We are neighbors and also have common acquaintances now. What do you say?"

I look at him, "OK we can be friends. Thanks for understanding."

"Prachi, I haven't forgotten our time together. And that was the best time of my life. So yes, my intention will always be to have you in my life. But if you don't want that then at least we can be friends, right?"

I can't hide my shocked expression from him. I knew he was direct and confident, but sometimes it was hard to show my emotions around him. I decided to stay quiet. Sometimes silence helps in handling situations much better.

4

Prachi- Brewing up a storm

We reached the apartment where I was staying. It feels like I should invite him over, but my inner voice scares me and it will make things more complicated. "Thank you for dropping me. How far do you stay?"

"I just stay in the opposite apartment building," he replies.

Again, this shocks me. "How long have you been staying in this apartment?" I ask, my brows turning into a frown.

"For almost 6 years," his answer makes my jaw drop. "Isn't it weird? We have been staying so close to each other for such a long time and we never crossed paths."

I look out the window and say, "Maybe we are not meant to be." I unlock my seat belt and get out of his car. He comes out of the driver's side and stands near me. "Sweet dreams Prachi"

I wish him the same with a polite smile and get inside the apartment.

Once I enter the building and enter the elevator, my heartbeat starts to slow. It was shocking for me to get to know that he has been my neighbor for the past 3 years. And yet I got to meet him in Goa. What are the chances of that happening? All these coincidences are making me confused.

I freshened up and went to bed. I could not sleep and kept tossing and turning for an hour. The thought of Arjun living across my street made me anxious which was not a good sign.

I got out of bed and went to my balcony to get some fresh air. While looking at the city's bright lights, I was in a deep dilemma about how to handle Arjun. Cause he had made it very clear that he was looking for something more like dating. But will I be able to keep the friendship level with him ever? Every time he is near me, my senses go wild.

At the same time, I got a text. It was from an unknown number.

You look damn sexy in those pajama shorts. <3

What the hell? I immediately realized someone could see me on the balcony. I went inside my room and replied to the text.

Who is this??

It made me anxious, thinking I might have some creep living across me. One of the weirdos who see across every day holding a binocular as we see in movies. A text came through in a minute.

Arjun

What the hell? He can see me through his balcony! In the moment of my panic, another text appears, making a ding.

I rattle you a lot. But even then, you look beautiful.

God! This guy knows how to get on my nerves. I replied immediately, saying,

Since when have you started behaving like a creep? And since how long have you been seeing me like this?

My brain was frying right now with the heat of my anger. How dare he? And since when does he have my number? Did he know all this time that I lived across from him? Another question comes to my mind... Did he know me before we met in Goa?

My phone started ringing, getting me back to reality. It was his number, and my temper skyrocketed. I received the call, and my first question was, "How long have you known me?"

He replies saying, "You don't want to know the answer. Tell me something, what's keeping you awake tonight?"

I see that he has lost his mind. "You don't need to know the answer," I repeated in the same tone as his. "Arjun, I don't know what you are doing or what is it that you want. But I must tell you something in advance, I don't like people who try to manipulate me or deceive me in any way. So if you want to be my friend then please keep things clean between us."

I was so angry I disconnected the call. I was fuming and pacing in my room. I noticed the curtains of my room to the balcony were open, and I immediately closed them. This guy is going to get me killed. As I tried to calm myself and was failing miserably, the intercom of my apartment started ringing. I clicked and asked, while my security guard said, "Madam, someone named Arjun is here to meet. And he is

saying it is important."

I wanted answers, and I knew I would be restless till I got them. So I asked the guard to send him up. I go to my wardrobe, take out an overcoat to wear, and open my main door. Arjun comes out of the elevator wearing casual track pants and a loose black t-shirt. His biceps were on full display, and his abs were trying to fight their way out of the t-shirt. I can't believe how handsome he is. He stood at my apartment entrance, and I looked him in the eye. He looked very confident and said, "Hi."

"Hi again. Come in."

He entered and scanned the living room. Taking in the interior as if he were always curious. Then he turned towards me and scanned me from top to bottom. As if he is trying to see the changes in me in the last year. I gesture for him to take a seat.

I didn't know what to say and what to ask. My brain was jelly after seeing him. "Arjun, can we have an honest and mature discussion?"

He looked into my eyes and nodded. "How long have you known me?" I asked.

His face hardened, "Three years."

"How? When? I don't understand." I started blabbering.

He was still looking at me, "It is a long story, but I want to assure you I am not a stalker. I just... You can say, fate has been bringing you in front of me from time to time."

I stayed quiet for a while. He looks around my apartment.

I moved into this apartment somewhere around three years ago. I guess Arjun has known me since then. There cannot be any other explanation for this.

God! He makes me mute with his handsome face and strong personality. How can anyone handle this kind of hotness? We both look at each other for a while. Then Arjun breaks the ice, "Prachi, how about we start fresh here? Making you angry is not on my priority list; believe me on that. How about I make it up to you by taking you out for dinner next week."

"You mean like a date?" I whispered.

"You can name it anything you want. I don't believe in labeling each and everything." he smiled at me slowly.

"I don't think that is a good idea. We should keep our friendship to a casual level." I replied to him even though my heart was screaming inside my head to say yes.

He looked at me with a serious expression and finally stood up and said, "I think I should leave now. I wanted to make sure your blood pressure was on the correct level," He chuckled. He came near me, stood pretty close, and I stopped breathing. He finally turned around and started walking towards the door. I walked behind him. Before he got on the elevator, he stood next to me and touched my face gently. He said, "I want you to stop resisting and release your inhibitions."

The whole time I was not breathing. So he feels it too. The pull and attraction that exists between both of us. I imagined him kissing me and me licking his abs vividly. He was breathing as hard as me. I was almost leaning to kiss him, but he let his hands fall from my cheeks. He whispered in my ears in a husky voice, "You keep running as long as you want, sweetheart. I'll keep chasing you!". He moves inside the elevator. And I was standing there staring at him with an open mouth.

What the hell just happened? Was I about to kiss him? And it was for sure that with Arjun, it would never have stopped at the just kiss.

5

Arjun- The chasing begins

I left Prachi's apartment and walked toward mine. I was going to kiss her, and I knew she wanted to kiss me as well as how she was leaning toward me. But she would have regretted it later. And I didn't want her to regret any part of her life with me. Somehow she has become my obsession. That day in Goa, when she left me near the beach, it hurt me to the core. I feel like something very wrong has happened with her in a past relationship. She is running from me now. She has trust issues and emotional baggage. But it is a fact that from the moment she left me standing near the beach, I haven't been able to get her out of my mind. And I am not going to stop until she is mine.

The time I spent with her in Goa was enough to tell me that I needed her in my life. It devastated me when she left, saying she was not looking to get involved with anyone. I wish I could tell her how much I feel for her.

It was not a coincidence that I happened to make my new home in Jabalpur. But yeah, it happened exactly as I wanted. Since my parents were more than happy to move back to our hometown and spend their time there happily.

When I told them I wanted to move back to Jabalpur, it got them excited as hell, and in my heart, I felt a bit guilty. I wanted to move there for Prachi, but somehow my parents got lucky with my decision. Being in the real estate business gave me easy access to the opposite land available from Prachi's home.

I need to come clean to my parents for real now. I need to go back to Jabalpur tomorrow.

The next morning, I reached Jabalpur with Rahul and Sameera. Both my siblings are my best friends and my confidants. But they are also extremely annoying. There is nothing that I ever hide from them. Once you reach a certain age, you tend to lose friends and start to bond with

family because you realize they are the most important people in the world. Except for Avisek, he is my best friend. I miss him a lot these days. But since he decided to join the Navy, I hardly get to see him. Plus, it isn't easy to contact him most of the time, given his job description.

I enter the house and find my parents sitting in the garden. I designed the house according to each family member's needs and convenience. My parents love the new garden with lawn chairs. I sit near them, and my mother passes me the apple slices she cut for my Dad. I smile at her. "I need to talk to you about something," I look at them with a blank face. They look startled and wait for me to begin.

"There was a reason I asked all of us to move back to Jabalpur. And the reason stays in front of our house."

My mother smiles at me and asks, "Is it Prachi?"

I nod, and she gives me a full, happy smile. I understand her sentiments. My parents gave up on the idea of me ever getting married. I am 32 years old, and for the past 7 years, I have immersed myself in work. After everything that happened with my ex-girlfriend, I never thought I would even think about any other girl. But since the day I saw Prachi, she got me mesmerized. And somehow, she came in front of me every single day. The only problem was that I was oblivious to her. She never even looked in my direction. And for the record, she never looked at anyone. I guess she was always in her world, and I am desperate to know that world of hers.

My father looked at me with concern in his eyes, "How do you know her?"

I told them the whole story, and they listened to me patiently. After I finished my story, they were quiet for a very long time.

It was like they knew something that I didn't. I asked them what they thought about it. My father asked me a question that put me in shock, "What do you know about her past?".

I didn't know what to answer because I don't know what happened with Prachi in the past, but I have always been curious. I shook my head, letting them know that I had no clue.

My father then told me the whole thing. "Prachi's parents are very concerned about her. She is hardly interested in anyone or anything other than her work. She has achieved success with too much hard work in a short time and since she is a single child, she is lonely. They are considering getting her married but don't want to force her into anything. It seems she was in a relationship a few years back. And since she was very young at that point, she couldn't realize that the guy was hampering her emotional health. She got abused emotionally and was so drained out that she lost her confidence. Her parents didn't know anything about all this at that point. One time she found the guy with some other girl and after that, she realized what was happening to her. She lost faith in her judgment and that is the reason she decided she is never going to be in a relationship anymore."

I asked, "How do you know all this?"

"We have become friends with the family. Her parents are very good people and are very decent. We talk about a lot of things. And we were wondering if you both would be a perfect match. If you want we can take it further ahead."

God knows how I became so lucky to have them as my parents, but it is for sure that I am the luckiest person in this world. I went back to my room and freshened up.

6

Prachi- Entering the cage

Three months later

I am sitting in front of a mirror in a house that feels more like a cage. I am dolled up in the gorgeous lehenga that Sameera designed. The beautiful matching ornaments are sparkling as much as the stars in the sky. I look like a queen. But I feel like a prisoner. The pearl droplets trying to fall from my eyes are just making me madder about the whole situation. And more than anything, I am mad at Arjun for making my life a fucking hell from which I can never go back. I am somewhat angry with my parents as well.

I am feeling my bones vibrating in my body. Seriously in this 21st-century era as well, people are so damn adamant about getting a girl married. If she is not married, a hell-storm will begin on earth. Women are getting married even when they don't want to. When will we get to live our lives on our terms? Ria left me in this room with a sympathetic look on her face. She didn't even dare to say anything to me. I think, she also knew I had lashed out at her if she had opened her smart mouth. She just hugged me and left me alone. I am losing control over myself at this point cause I don't know what to do.

I hear the door of the room opening, and my eyes go straight to see who it is. I find Arjun standing in front of me, looking handsome in a suit. I can't believe even when I am livid; I find him handsome. And at the same thought, the tears that I was trying to hold back fell on their own. I can hardly see his face anymore. But I don't bother anymore. I want him to see how miserable I am feeling. I want him to feel how helpless he made me feel due to this situation. He manipulated me into this marriage.

He comes near me and gives me a tissue, but being a stubborn bitch I behave as if he does not exist. He moves around the chair; I am sitting on and kneeling. He wipes my tears and kisses my forehead. But he didn't say anything, and I think he also knew well not to push me right now.

I don't know what came into his mind, but he started removing all my ornaments very carefully.

He went to my bags, removed a tank top and pajama shorts, and handed them to me. He also removed my makeup by taking a makeup remover from my makeup bag. And the whole time, I kept crying. He went to the bathroom, and after a few minutes, he took my hand and pulled me towards the bathroom. I thought he was going crazy if he thought I would go into the bathroom with him. But when I entered the bathroom, I saw a bathtub, and he had drawn me a bath. He looked at me and said, "You should freshen up and take a bath. Please don't lock the bathroom.

I don't want you to pass out inside and get locked. I will be outside if you need anything." And he left. The moment he left the bathroom, I fell to the floor of the bathroom and started crying again.

After a while, I removed my clothes and got into the bathtub. My eyes were feeling heavier after so much crying.

I was almost dozing when I heard a knock on the bathroom door. "Can I come in just for a minute?" asked Arjun. I made a grunted noise, and he came inside. I was inside

the bathtub full of bubbles. He brought me a glass of bourbon and handed it to me. He was wearing a T-shirt and shorts.

I took it from him and drank the whole thing in one shot. He went out and brought the bottle and filled my glass. "Drink it slowly. I just want to talk to you."

I glared at him, "You know, I am not going to forgive you for doing this. It's not that I hate you or something. I liked you so much that I was willing to let go of my walls. But the fact that you stole that decision from me, I will never forgive you."

He looked at me with hurt all over his face, "Prachi you know very well that you would never have stepped out of your walls. And I didn't force you into this marriage. If not for me, eventually you would have married someone else just for the sake of your parents. But I love you and I need you in my life. I can live with your anger and grudge rather than not having you in my life at all. So forgive me for becoming a selfish dick. But I just took the opportunity to avoid future regrets. I didn't want to sit in my room thinking that if I had tried anything harder we would have been together. NO! I love you and I know you love me too. The connection we both have is very rare and you know it too. So you can run away from it as long as you want but I am not going to. I am an opportunist, I grab what I want in life."

I was so emotional at that point I just started crying again. He sat on the bathtub's edge, "If you stay any longer in here, you will fall sick and become a prune. Come out of the tub or I will carry you out on my own."

I looked away from him. My head was hurting so bad that I couldn't see straight. My eyes were starting to close. At the same moment, I felt carried away. Then I remembered I hadn't eaten anything the whole day. I think Ria gave me a glass of juice. The bourbon and the tears went straight to my brain. I knew I was wet and naked, but at that point, I was not in a state to do anything about it. But I was aware of everything in my surroundings. Arjun carried me out of the tub, wrapped me in a towel, and took me to bed. He made me wear a tank top and pajama shorts and tucked me in the blanket. He was completely wet as he took me out of the tub wearing his clothes. He went somewhere, and in a few minutes, he returned wearing boxers.

He got in the blanket and spooned me. He caressed my forehead, "Go to sleep Prachi. You have your whole life to be angry and hate me." I closed my eyes and felt a kiss on my forehead while I went into the darkness.

7

Arjun- My fucking heart

It feels like someone has punched through my chest and tried to pull my heart out of my body. Seeing the person you love in so much pain is the most horrible feeling anyone can ever have. Especially, if you are the reason for the tears. The moment I entered the room, her eyes started overflowing.

She cried so much that the painful voice coming out of the bathroom tore my heart into pieces. But I am still hopeful that she will see the love in my eyes one day. That day she will understand why I did whatever I did.

She looks so fragile while sleeping. Holding her in my arms feels like the best thing in the world. But she is still quivering in her sleep and it is too stressful for even me to handle. I want to give her the whole world.

I need to fix this for both of us. I don't know how but this is not how I ever imagined my marriage. Hell, I never thought that my wife would cry her eyes out on our first night. But even I am mature enough to know, it was in the cards. I am the reason for her tears.

Tomorrow I will show her why we are both best for each other. I will make her feel for me again, and I will fix my marriage. I hope she will stop crying by tomorrow morning. I have never seen her like this and never want to see her like this ever again.

I will have to talk to Ria. Maybe she can help me out. Prachi has major insecurity issues, and I need to dig deeper to fix everything between us. I need to gain her trust in the first place. I need to make her feel safe whenever she is with me.

I looked at her one more time, and I entered oblivion while holding her tight in my arms.

I felt a pull in my sleep. I was so tired that I didn't want to open my eyes at all, but I felt like someone was struggling to get out of somewhere. I opened my eyes slowly and saw Prachi struggling to get out of my hold. Her eyes were throwing daggers at me, "Let me go!" Something started pushing me from inside; I flipped and made her lie on the bed with me hovering over her. I looked into her eyes; she was a vision. Each feature on her face and body is ravishing. Even though her eyes looked puffy and her face looked dull after so much crying, she still took my breath away. "Never ask me again to let you go. I will let you live in whatever way you want, and I will support you and be there for you throughout my life. But I will never let you go."

She blinked at me. I didn't want to get out of bed as I was still tired. I checked the time on my watch, and it was only 5 AM. I groaned, "What the hell are you going to do at this ungodly hour?"

She replied, "This is when I wake up every morning you dumbass!"

What? Is she kidding? Who wakes up at 5 AM?

As soon as I freed her arms from my hold she sprinted to the bathroom and locked herself. After a few minutes, I heard the shower running. I was fidgeting because I didn't know how she was going to behave today, and I could not go back to sleep again. After a while, she came out of the bathroom and went inside her closet. I have stocked the place with clothes for her. I asked Sameera to buy clothes as per Prachi's preference, and she went wild with them. Prachi came out of the closet and stood in front of me by folding her arms, "If you don't mind me asking where can I keep my clothes from my bags? The closet is full it seems."

"Those are your clothes. I got it stocked for you. So what you like, you can keep. The rest you can remove and you can keep your clothes from the bag also in the same," I replied to her. Her eyes went wide. "Have you lost your mind? Who keeps so many clothes? And why did you buy so much for me? Actually, why did you buy so many clothes for me in the first place?" She was looking so cute being angry at me. I have lost my mind; even in this situation, I am aroused. She is angry with me, and even that is turning me on. Only if she could hear my thoughts right now I think she would kick me in the balls.

"Are you even listening to me?" She asked.

"If you are planning on standing here in a robe and shouting at me, I guess it is obvious for my brain to start dreaming something else, isn't it? I must say if it could go my way I would pull you into this bed and not let you go till you are not in the condition to walk," I smiled at her. This made her go red. God! I could eat her up and make her moan my name right now.

She looked at me as if I had gone crazy. She stomped to her closet again and came out wearing a red dress. It was, I guess, a gown kind of suit with a simple dupatta. Sameera has done a great job. Prachi always wears simple clothes though she wears all kinds of colors. I have never seen her wearing anything with too much print, designs, or sparkly. I don't think I will ever get tired of looking at her beautiful face.

She glanced at me once with angry eyes and went out of our room. I checked the time again, and it was 6 AM. I finally woke up from my bed and got freshened up. I wore my joggers and T-shirt and thought of going for a run.

8

Prachi- Pleading the predator

The man had the nerve to look at me like that. I would have punched him in the balls if I were not intoxicated and vulnerable last night. I am so confused with the turmoil of feelings I am going through right now. First of all, the things Arjun said last night to me when I was in the bathtub are still lingering in my head. He indeed created a situation where I had to marry him. But he is also right that eventually, my parents would have created this kind of emotional drama with someone else. Since I broke up with my ex-boyfriend Madhav, my parents have been worrying about me a lot. I told them from time to time that I didn't want to get married. I didn't want to be with anyone, which made them more anxious. As I am the only child and we are not very close with any of our relatives, they think that I will be all alone after they are gone. My parents fell in love and eloped together. Both families didn't approve of their love because of caste and financial status issues. They took matters into their own hands and got married. They have few good friends but no relatives or family members.

Recently, they bonded with Arjun's parents, who became our neighbors 4 months back. And it seems my parents have been venting all their worries to them. Arjun's parents approached me about the marriage of Arjun with me. I was not shocked because this is normal in our culture. What shocked me was how my father started blackmailing me. He said they both would leave the house if I didn't marry Arjun. I was angry as hell. What surprised me more was that they thought Arjun and his family were the best I could ever get. Since they live across the street, I will still stay close to them. I fought a lot with them. I even went to Arjun for help.

Two months back

After the day my parents created so much chaos about marriage, I thought of asking Arjun for help. I texted Arjun on a Thursday morning.

Hey,

Are you in the office right now?

I waited for a few minutes, and his reply came through.

Hey,

This is a pleasant surprise. I was just now thinking about you. Yes, I am in the office.

I thought talking in person would be better.

Can we meet today? I can come by your office.

Instantly his reply came saying,

Sure. Let's have lunch together. I will order something nice.

As much as that sounded nice, I was not in the mood to handle his flirtatious talk for now.

Okay. I will reach around noon. I replied.

I was not in the mood to work. Sarita kept lining my meetings, and I was half-mindedly attending all. I asked to clear my calendar for the day as I needed to be very calm while requesting Arjun's help.

I reached his office around 11:30 AM and didn't want to look too anxious. I needed coffee to calm myself, so I went to the nearby café and grabbed my americano with extra espresso shots.

I sipped my coffee while still standing outside his office. When it was almost 11:50 AM, I entered the building. I checked with the receptionist, and she took me to the top floor of the building. And they took me to Arjun's office. I knocked, and he asked me to come in. I found Arjun sitting at his desk wearing a fine suit when I entered. As soon as his eyes fell on me, he stood from his desk and came to stand near me. He smelled incredible. Come on, Prachi, focus!

He greeted me, saying, "Hey. How are you doing?" A splitting smile on his face would make anyone smile even if they are under a mountain load of stress over their shoulder.

I replied to him politely, "Hello. I am good. How are you?"

"Amazing that I got to see you now. Let's sit on the couch."

He called someone and asked to bring food and juice. While he was doing that, I took a look at his office. Even though it looked clean and posh it looked out of order. As if many things are out of place. My OCD makes me exhausted at times. He came and sat on the nearby couch.

I couldn't speak any words for a long time. I know he likes me, and that is the reason he might have said yes to the proposal. But I need to convince him that marrying me will not be good for both of us.

"So what opened my luck today for you to come to visit me?" he asked, breaking the silence.

I was so nervous that I could not frame my sentences properly, "I guess you already know about the fact that our parents are talking about our marriage."

He supported his chin on his fist looked at me with a smile for a while, and replied, "Yes."

A single word.

"So, what do you think about it?" I asked.

"From the way you are broaching the subject, it seems you are nervous to talk about it with me."

At the same time, someone knocked on the door, and Arjun asked them to come in. Two guys came inside with pizza boxes and juice cans. Arjun passed me a small pizza box and a juice can. It was surprising that a billionaire like him would order a pizza to eat.

"You can say that. Do you like eating pizza from this shop or you are not that picky?"

"I love eating pizza, especially from this shop. Also, I remember you saying that pizza was your comfort food. So, I thought we could have a nice pizza today. I hope it is okay for you," he replied.

"Yeah, it is okay. Well, what have you told at your home about the marriage proposal?" I asked and took a slice of the pizza.

He looked into my eyes and sighed. When he opened his mouth to say the next words, "It was me who asked my parents to consider the proposal." I choked on the pizza that was in my mouth. Somehow, I would die eating my favorite food, at least I thought.

I didn't know how to react and what to say, but my temper got the best of me. I worked so hard to keep my temper issue in check but damn this guy. He makes me mad and horny at the same time. I am shaking with anger right now, yet I want to bite his lips until the blood comes out of them. And I can punch him in his throat later.

"I don't want to get married, Arjun. And you know this, I don't want to be in a relationship. And you always give me this feeling that you like me and want me to take things ahead between us. If that is true, why would you send a marriage proposal? I mean wouldn't you want me to feel the same as you and be with you because I want to?" I was trying very hard to keep my voice to a least as it was his office.

His face appeared as if he wanted to thrust me to the couch and keep me there till he got his way with me. What the fuck is wrong with me? "Prachi, believe it or not, I don't think you will ever change your mind about giving us a chance. You are too much of a coward to do so. Plus, even if it wasn't me when someone else might have sent a proposal to your parents, they would have considered that as well. And you would have married someone else for sure, in the end, to make your parents happy. So I thought why can't I be that guy?"

"How are you so sure that I will agree to marry anyone at all to make my parents happy?"

"If that was not the case, we would not be sitting here, talking to each other right now. Another way around I would have received a rejection of the proposal by now." I must say the guy had the balls to do something like this. I understand him now well. He is one of those guys who use their brains and intelligence to the most for their benefit. He has already observed and figured out my parents and my weakness toward them. He knows I will never be the reason for my parent's unhappiness.

"Plus, the fact that I am staying opposite your house is a winning point for me. Prachi think about it. If you agree to marry me, I will let you live your life as you want without any interference from my side. I will support you in every way you want. You can stay near your parents as you are staying right now. We already know how compatible we are with each other. We can lead a happy life. And the main thing is I am not a stranger. We have this weird need for each other, doesn't matter how much you deny it but it's there. Don't you think it is better than marrying someone you don't know at all?" He was whispering and trying to calm me down.

But I was feeling betrayed. I know what he was saying was all sensible talk. But the fact is I was hoping if we ever get together, it will be very natural between us. I knew the attraction between us was wild and primal. I was hoping one day if l gave in, things would proceed naturally. Since he started this marriage proposal nonsense, he took away the most magical thing that could have happened between us. I already knew I couldn't refuse this proposal. My parents have already given me the ultimatum. But I thought he would help me out.

My eyes started to water, and I didn't want to cry in front of him. I felt helpless. "I came here to ask for your help. But it seems you are the reason for my problem right now." I tried to hold together my emotions, took my bag, and immediately walked out of his office. And he didn't even try stopping me.

Back to the present

I went out of the room to the house's main hall and moved towards the lawn. I found my mother-in-law and father-in-law sitting there on lawn chairs drinking tea. I took their blessings, and my mother-in-law kissed my forehead. My father-in-law asked someone to bring my black coffee. I have to admit; that my in-laws are very nice.

My father-in-law said, "You should go and meet your parents. They must be missing you. And don't feel obligated to do anything in a certain way. Just do whatever makes you happy. You are a part of this family now. Just like Sameera, your happiness matters to us." He caressed my head once and went inside the house.

I felt a bit grateful. My only problem was Arjun. I have to stay away from him as much as possible.

9

Prachi- Guilty conscience

I walk towards my house to meet my parents. I don't know why but am very nervous and sad. Because it doesn't matter how angry I feel right now at my parents, I love them the most in this world. And they have no one other than me. I stand outside the gates of my own house. I felt someone holding my hand from behind, and I didn't need to look at who it was. His mere presence is enough to make me feel jittered. He looks straight and says, "It is the first day of our marriage. We need to go meet them together. And Prachi, I know you are angry with me and your parents. But I just want to say, you can put all your anger on me and keep all the love for your parents. I can be your punching bag but let's not ruin this day for them. They must have dreamed a lot about this day for you."

I look at his face and see his genuine care and admiration for my parents. Somehow I melted a bit inside for him. My throat feels heavy, "Let's just go inside and meet them." I open the gate and go inside while Arjun holds my hand and walks beside me. I open the door and find my parents sitting in the hall. As soon as they see us, they come near us, and we give our respects to them by touching their feet. I try to give them a genuine smile, but my heart and eyes start watering. My mother kisses Arjun's cheeks and gives him blessings while my father puts his hand on my head and caresses me.

We go inside and sit in the dining area where our cook Ramu uncle comes with delicious food. Rava upma, chutney, and lots of sweets. By looking at it all, I knew my Mom had made it all. I miss Ria, "Where is Ria?" At the same moment, She sprints down and hugs me from behind. I hug her back and feel a bit relieved. First time in years, I understood the value of this girl. I actually can't survive without her in my life, and today I felt it was the right time to express this feeling because I needed her. "Ria, I just want to say this to you, you have become a part of my life, and I think I can't survive without you in it. You have helped me achieve the heights of success and gave me all the support and nudge I ever needed. So thank you." Ria is a sucker for emotional talk, and I should have known she would start crying like a small kid.

I saw Arjun watching me with an expression I couldn't understand, maybe admiration. I also saw how he talked with my parents, and that too with so much ease. As if he had known them for a very long time. I guess by watching this, any girl would melt a little bit.

After breakfast, I was not sure what to do. Normally, I work in any free time I get. But today, it felt weird. I mean, I don't think anyone works the next day of their marriage. Plus, I have handed over all my work to Ria and the rest of the team for two weeks. And usually, it is Ria or Sarita who tells me what I will be doing the whole day. I am feeling so restless; a day without any purpose is torture.

I need a purpose for these two weeks. Oh Yes! I can have the best purpose, and it will make me so happy. Mr. Arjun

Dixit is going to pay hell for getting married to me. Because from today onwards, I will make his life a living hell.

As I was making plans for the next few days, my father asked, "Are you both packed for your honeymoon?" and I was like, "What?"

I was looking at him and Arjun with an open mouth. My father said again, "I have booked a honeymoon trip for both of you to Thailand. I told Ria and Arjun. It was a surprise for you."

I was speechless. No! Noo! Nooo! I can't go on a honeymoon trip with Arjun right now. I mean, it isn't easy to stay in the same room with him. At the same time, Arjun replied to my father when I was still in shock, "Yes, we have done the packing and are ready to go. We will be leaving after lunch. And thank you so much for planning this trip for us. I am sure we will have a good time." Arjun was perfectly smiling at my parents and was looking at me with a side-eye.

I stood from my place, "Ria can you please come to the office for 5 mins? I want to transfer a few files to you before I leave." Ria gave me a questioning look but did as I asked. I went up to my office and closed the office door after Ria entered. I looked at her and asked, "Did you know

about this trip?" She nods. "Why didn't you tell me? I could have done something to avoid it. You know how I am feeling about this marriage. Didn't it occur to you that after going through all this nonsense, I might want to dig into work?"

Ria looks helpless and guilty, "Prachi, I know this whole situation is difficult for you. But it is what it is! You married him. And you got married to a guy who loves you a lot. You both have amazing chemistry and connection. Your parents love him. Both families are so happy. He is good looking and you also like him and you can't deny it."

She stayed quiet for a minute, "Your father was so happy and excited while looking for honeymoon packages. He wanted to make you happy. He asked me not to tell you about it as he planned it as a surprise for you. Prachi, do you have any idea how lucky you are? I know a few things didn't go your way. But your parents love you so much. You have married a good guy and his family is also amazing. You have good people in your life. Not everyone is that blessed."

I know what she is saying is true. I know how all this must look to her. She is an orphan without a family, parents, or anyone to say her own. But I thought at least she understood my pain. I looked at Ria; my eyes started watering, "So you think I should forgive Arjun for everything and start playing Happy House?"

Ria came and sat near me, "Prachi, I am not saying that you should forgive Arjun. I am just saying stop being angry with everyone and every situation. I know and understand what you are going through right now. Your relationship with Arjun is different. You can see how both family members are feeling. How much they love you and how much they adore you. Go on this trip and enjoy yourself. You always wanted to go to Thailand. So enjoy the moment."

I didn't know what to do. Being with Arjun 24x7 in a beautiful place. It is going to be damn hard.

10

Arjun- First step to the right

Prachi and I returned to our room after breakfast with her parents. She was visibly red, with anger oozing out of her. The moment we entered the room, she went inside her wardrobe. After a while, she came out and sat on the couch. She somewhat looked calm now. I went and sat opposite her. I wanted to sit near her, but I thought better not try my luck right now.

She looked at me, and I melted with just the look. The struggle within her was visible. She again looked down and back at me, "Arjun, I don't know what to say but is it necessary for us to go on this trip? I mean can't we go to Bangalore and pretend like we are in Thailand."

I smiled, "Sure we can do that. But what are you going to do when our family asks us to send pictures, or what if they video-call us? You know our families are like that."

She stayed quiet. I knew how to make it simple for her, "Prachi, how about we go on the trip, and you enjoy it your way? If you want me to stay out of your way, then I will. I will shadow you. We can think of it as a vacation to relax from our hectic lifestyle. We both are always so busy with work that we hardly ever get time to relax. What do you say?"

She looks towards the window, "As if I have any other option. Anyways, how am I going to pack things in such a short time?"

I tell her, "Sameera has already packed all things for you. It is inside your wardrobe storage." She goes inside again and pulls her trolley out. She opens the trolley and slaps her hand on her forehead. Someone knocks on our bedroom door. I open it, and Sameera sprints inside, "Prachi, oh, you found the trolley. I wanted to give you the list of things that I have packed for you so that you can find all things easily." Sameera was smiling to her ears. Prachi was looking hopeless, "Sameera, I am going just for a week, it looks like you have packed for a whole month." Sameera was so excited. She was half jumping, "I checked your itinerary for your trip. I have kept all your clothes according to the places you are going to visit. Also, I have kept a few extra clothes in case of any mishaps or emergencies."

Prachi stood up and went near Sameera. She touched both sides of her shoulders and said, "Sameera sweetheart, you know I adore you so much and value our friendship a lot, right?"

Sameera smiled, "Of course, you know I like you too."

To which Prachi made a serious face, "Then why are you trying to make me hate you?"

Sameera laughed, "Come on Prachi, don't worry about it. I have chosen all the clothes as per your liking. And it is better to pack extra, just in case of new plans. I hope you have a good time on your honeymoon. Also, think of this as me saying thank you for getting me new clients and connections. Because of you, I have received new clients and I am enjoying working with them."

Prachi's face softens on this, "I am happy for you. I wish to see your fashion line in Lakme Fashion Week one day." Sameera hugs her, kisses my cheeks, and says, "Have a good time bro." And then she leaves.

Prachi looks at me and says, "I'll go get changed. By the way, can you please tell me our travel plans?"

"Well, we are going directly to Thailand from here on our private plane. Then we will check in to our hotel."

"Okay, thanks.", She gets inside the washroom to get changed. I am nervous; I have been anxious about this trip. I was damn sure that she would find a way to cancel it. I need to talk to Ria before going on this trip. This is the best time as Prachi will be busy getting ready. I go back to her house and find her in Prachi's office. I knock on the door and she looks surprised and asks me to come in. I enter and take a chair opposite her.

Ria says, "Hey, Arjun. What are you doing here? Aren't you supposed to get ready to leave for your honeymoon?"

I look at her and hesitate, "Yeah, I am ready. I need to talk to you before I leave. I wanted to ask about Prachi and you are the only person who can help me out. Ria, you already know Prachi is not happy with this wedding because of the way it happened. And I agree it was completely wrong on my part. But I love her and I want her to be happy. I just did whatever I did because I didn't want to lose her. I am trying to win her back but Prachi has major trust issues. She hardly talks to me and I don't know how to win her trust. Do you think you can help me out in this?"

Ria's face becomes pale, "Arjun you know Prachi will kill me if she gets to know you are even discussing this with me right? She is very private with her feelings and thoughts. She had a very hard time trusting me in the initial days. But somehow we became a good fit for each other work-wise and well as in the friendship department."

I try to persuade her a bit more, "Ria I love her and I want her to be happy. But right at this moment, I am the reason for her distress and unhappiness. It is painful for me to see her like this. I want her normal self back. When it comes to love, I am okay if she never has the same feelings for me."

Ria looks at me for a while and then looks out the sliding glass door. "I also want her to be happy Arjun. She is my best friend and my only backbone. I can't tell you how to win her back.

But I can tell you something which makes her the way she is. But you will let her tell this to you from her side. If she somehow finds out that I told you, she will kick me out of her life. So, you have to promise to keep it to yourself."

"I promise you that this will stay within us."

Ria begins, "Well her last relationship has made her rigid. He was from her college and she loved him more than anything. She made a hell of a lot of sacrifices to be with him. She thought he loved her as well but one day changed her life completely. She came to visit her parents here for a few days. While returning she went a day early to surprise him and found him fucking her friend in their bedroom. It shattered her from the inside. When she confronted both of them, her friend started getting aggressive and slapped her. And her ex-boyfriend laughed. When she tried to fight back with her friend, Madhav her ex-boyfriend came between and manhandled Prachi. Since both of them were living together, they maintained a joint bank account. She bought all the furniture and appliances for the house. But he kicked her out that day from the apartment and took all the money that they both saved in the joint account. It is a good thing, she kept a separate bank account for emergencies and saved some money there. But for that particular moment, she was on the roads. She searched for a shared apartment in

Bangalore and luckily found one. She shifted there and since then she took a different path. She wrote her first book and published it. Then she resigned from her job and we started our company. And she never looked back. The problem is after that day she became a different person. What I heard from her parents, she was a lively and happy person. I was one of her roommates when she was living in the shared apartment. I had just graduated from college and was searching for a job while doing some part-time work. She used to live in the next room to me and, we became friends. She took me in her wing and I learned a lot from her."

I was speechless and didn't know what to say. My blood was boiling with anger for this guy. Ria brought me back to attention, "Arjun, she is angry with you because she is feeling betrayed somehow. And it will be very difficult for you to make things right."

I stood from my chair and gave a sad smile to Ria, "Thanks a lot Ria for helping me out here. At least I know now how to start making things good for her."

Ria smiled back, "Arjun I told you all this because I think you genuinely love her. So don't make me regret this. Prachi is someone I never want to lose in my life. But I also want her to be happy. So you better get on track and start fixing everything."

"I promise you I will fix it.", and left her office and went back to my house.

11

Prachi- The fucking emotions

I get changed into the clothes Sameera kept for me. It is a knee-length blue dress with angel sleeves. I thought of going and meeting both my and Arjun's parents before leaving for the trip.

As I was about to leave the room, Arjun entered. His face is full of emotions as if he is angry as well as sad at the same time. Out of impulse, I ask, "Are you okay? You look disturbed."

He looks at me for a while and then looks down. Did someone say something to upset him? I should be happy, but I don't feel happy with him being sad.

"Nothing. I am worried about a few work things. Nothing major.", He is lying, and I can feel something is bothering him, but I shut up. Who cares whatever is keeping him down, right?

We go to the dining hall to have lunch with Arjun's parents. Sameera and Rahul also joined. Rahul comes to me and kisses my cheeks, and I smile. Rahul and I have developed a friendly relationship in the last few months. He is a fun person to be around. He has this aura that makes everyone feel up to the beat. But Arjun is glaring at Rahul. He looks jealous. What the hell? He is jealous of his brother. This man has serious issues.

We all chat and eat a nice meal. I must say, this feels good. I haven't felt this homey in anyone's presence ever. Arjun, who is sitting right beside me, is fidgeting. I know I shouldn't feel this concern towards him given the situation between us. But somehow, I want to know what is going on in his devil kind of head.

After we all finished eating, everyone wished us a good trip. We both go to our room, collect our belongings, and step out of the house. My parents have also come to see us off. I see them happy, and it somersaults me. Ria is there too. I hug everyone and get inside the car.

We sit quietly, and Arjun has not looked at me once the whole ride. We reached the airport and get boarded the jet. I must say the jet looks quite luxurious. We sit right beside each other. I brought three books with me to read on this trip. I couldn't get my laptop, so I had to get something to keep me busy.

After the flight takes off, I don't know why but I keep looking at Arjun. He is wearing faded jeans and a black t-shirt while keeping his denim jacket on the side. He is so handsome and beautiful.

He has a ruggedness in his whole personality. His jawline is perfect. He is sitting with his eyes closed. Looks like he hadn't slept at all last night.

I want to reach out to hold his hand and ask him what is bothering him. But I remind myself that I am angry with him and shouldn't care about what is bothering him.

As if feeling my eyes on him, Arjun says, "I am not going to bite. At least not when you are angry with me. So, if you have something to say, then just say it, Prachi." He still has his eyes closed the whole time. How does he do that? I know we have this weird connection. We always feel

each other's presence before even coming eye to eye.

"It's just, that you look out of character. What happened when you came to the room before lunch?" I ask, keeping my tone nonchalant.

He opens his eyes and looks towards me while I look anywhere but at him. "Are you worried about me, baby? Because I could feel good with a kiss or two. Even a hug would be better." He gave me a wicked smile.

Ugh! This man is infuriating to the core. I glare at him and then take my book out and start reading. I could see him looking at me the whole time out of my peripheral vision. So I burst out with my words again, "Will you tell me what the problem with you is? Why are you behaving like this?"

He gives me a sad smile again, "I never thought our next vacation together would be like this. That's all. But don't worry about it. Enjoy reading your book. I'll take a nap."

His words registered with me; he is sad that we are going on our honeymoon, and I am not happy about it. Honestly, it makes me a bit sad too. But I can't ignore everything that happened and changed my life in a single air blow.

I go back to reading my book, and I slip into a deep nap somewhere in an hour.

12

Arjun- Agitation in paradise

Prachi slept so peacefully that I didn't feel like waking her up. Once we landed, I carried her in my arms and got off the plane. I wish things were different, but it will be fun from here onwards. I know one thing, and that is Prachi loves me too. She doesn't want to accept it right now. I thought of taking it easy and gentle with her till she came around. But the woman is so damn stubborn I have to do it the hard way again, like getting married to her.

I know I will jump into dangerous water, but at least it will be adventurous. Since I am already married to her, she can't run away from me anymore. And I was serious when I told her about being an opportunist. I take what I want in life, and intend to make her mine ultimately. I want her heart, her soul, her body, her brain. Her everything!

My crew member brought our luggage to the car. And I slid Prachi into the back seat and got inside on the other side. I thought of Prachi as a light sleeper, but I guess recently, she might not be sleeping well with the stress of marriage. After an hour, we reached the resort. When

Prachi opened her eyes and seemed confused about her environment, "Where are we? How did I get off the plane?"

God, she is adorable! "I carried you, of course. You passed out, and I didn't want to wake you. We have reached the resort now. Shall I carry you from here, or do you think you can walk on your own?" I smirked with an amused smile.

Her eyes immediately grew big, and her soft sleepy expression changed to an angry one. I laughed at how easily she gets triggered. She immediately got out of the car, grabbing her handbag like it was a weapon. She stomped towards the reception, and I followed her behind, getting a view of her curvy ass.

I went ahead of her and asked the receptionist to check us in. Meanwhile, the receptionist was eyeing me like I was her favorite candy giving me a coy smile. I peeked to my side and found Prachi watching the receptionist with a death glare with her lips in a thin line. I was hoping to see her react somehow, but I knew she would not show her emotions so easily. But that doesn't mean I can't have some fun, right?

After registering us, the receptionist asked me with a flirty smile, "Would you like to have some drinks sent to your room, Sir? A bottle of chilled champagne or wine? It looks like you could use it."

"A bottle of champagne will be good. Also, a bottle of scotch would be nice if you can arrange it." I gave her a soft smile. "Sure, Sir! I will have it sent to your room immediately. Your room is ready, and our staff will help you to your room now."

We move towards our room as the staff member helps us. Last time when we were moving towards a hotel room, things were so different. I was licking her neck and kissing her well. Is she also remembering those moments? But soon, I will have her in my arms.

As soon as we enter our room, Prachi gets a smile on her face. I follow her gaze and see why she is so mesmerized. The view from our room is fantastic. Our first destination was Ko Lipe.

We have our cottage with direct access to the beach. And the view is breathtaking. It is already evening, so people enjoy themselves on the beach with a bonfire and playing games.

I smiled at the thought of Prachi wearing a bikini and strolling around the beach. And at the same time, it occurred to me that she would be wearing a bikini! While all the guys will be admiring her beauty, I won't be able to hold her to me to save her from their prying eyes.

God! This is a mess.

Prachi opens the back door towards the beach while removing her heels and starts walking barefoot on the sand. At the same time, our Champagne arrives. I take two glasses fill both and remove my shoes. I carry both the glass and follow in Prachi's direction. She had finally taken place near the shore and was playing with sand sitting on the beach. I sat near her and handed her a glass. She looks at me with a look I cannot understand but clinks her glass with mine and drinks from it. "Did you bring the bottle with you?" she asks. I shook my head even though I wanted to tease her with a sarcastic reply.

She drinks slowly while her throat blobs, and I watch with a glooming look. Everything about her is seducing me. I wish I could ask her what she thinks, but I know better. I won't get a straight answer from her right now. So I look towards the crystal clear water and enjoy the breeze.

13

Prachi- Crumbling walls

Evening on a beach so beautiful is a privilege to witness. Our daily busy life is so different from what you experience by sitting in a beautiful place like this. Doing nothing but enjoying the view. It changes your perspective on life. What is more disturbing is Arjun sitting beside me doing the same.

It is weird cause this is how we met in Goa. The same way we are sitting right now, we have this tension. And I know it is because of me. I am angry with him, and I guess, to some extent, he is angry with me too. I look at him again, sitting here with me on the beach sand. He seems calm yet disturbed at the same time. It takes all kinds of restraining from me not to reach out to him, hold his hand, and soothe all his thoughts.

I get up from my place and walk towards the shore to dip my feet in the cool water. It is getting dark, and the moon is shining on the horizon. People are drinking and playing around. I go a little deeper into the water feeling the sand move beneath my feet. It feels like I am slipping into the water and want to take a dip in it. I look around and see many people playing in the water. I come out of the water and go in the direction of our room to change. Arjun's gaze follows me the whole time. I remove my dress as I am already wearing a bikini set inside. And take the champagne bottle with me to the beach and a towel from the bathroom. I move towards Arjun, and the moment he looks at me, his jaw drops. Okay, great. But, his jaw starts to tick upwards, looking at our surroundings. I don't know what he thinks, but I become bold with his reaction. I hand him the bottle, and he refills our glasses. I take the glass from him and drink it all in one swing. I put the glass on the sand and moved towards the water. I get inside the water, and the cool water makes me feel amazing. The water keeps swishing to my body, and I keep playing within. Suddenly, Arjun is by my side in the water in just a boxer. I looked towards where he was sitting and saw all his clothes lying there.

He comes near me, and I stop breathing cause I know I won't be able to push him away right now. I am craving him too much to do that. He takes my hand, and I let him move me deeper into the water. When we are neck-deep into the water, I see the moon's reflection over the water. Arjun holds me around my waist the whole time and stands behind me. It amazes me that he still remembers that I don't know how to swim, making me nervous about being this deep in water. But with him holding me secure, I enjoy being in his arms and the water moving over us. The moon's reflection falls on his face, making him look more handsome than ever.

After a while, he pulls me out of the water, and while holding my hand, he walks me towards our cottage. Somehow he has managed to get his clothes, our glasses, and the bottle as well. But after a while, I notice he is not taking me inside the cottage but rather another side of it.

Then I

find an open shower there. Arjun opens the tap, stands under it, and pulls me by his side. The water moves along our bodies and washes the saltiness and the sand from our skin. But the whole time, Arjun doesn't touch me in any way. Am I hoping for him to touch me? Why is it bothering me that he is being a gentleman?

After some time, he takes my hand, wraps me in the towel I brought before, and takes me inside the cottage. "Get changed, we can go have dinner. I have booked a table in a nice restaurant." He says while taking fresh clothes out of his luggage.

"Can we go to the walking street here instead? I have heard they have great street food there and it is famous too."

He looked at me furrowed, "You want to eat street food?"

"Well yeah! We eat in good restaurants all the time. But if you want to get the real taste of any cuisine, then you definitely should eat street food. They make the best. And since we are here, I thought we should eat the local food, you know, explore it well."

Arjun looks at me with confusion looming on his face. Did he plan something else that I have ruined or something?

I open my trolley bag and look for the clothes Sameera packed for me. She has wrapped all outfits in different plastic bags with the date and time written on them. I reached for the plastic bag dated for today. I opened it and found a black floral printed dress. It has a halter knotted neck style, and the length was above my knees and very lightweight. I put on my dress and dry my hair. With the humid weather, putting on any make-up was useless, so I put on a matte nude lipstick. I wear black wedge heels along with them and keep my hair open. Due to the humid climate, my hair has become a bit wavy, but somehow, it looks amazing.

I get out of the bathroom and find Arjun waiting for me. He is wearing denim shorts along with a light blue color loose half shirt. His biceps are on full display, and he looks dapper in it. He looks at me from top to bottom, and again his jaw ticks. I never understand why he does that. Does he not like my outfit? Well, hell with him. I like my dress and Sameera is good with the designs and outfits.

I tell him, "I hope you pay Sameera for designing this dress for me. She is amazing, by the way. From now on I am only going to wear dresses designed by her. I don't know how she does it, but she always keeps my comfort in priority and still makes the best dress for me."

Arjun smiles, "I will make sure to pay her for all the dresses 'cause you are right. She makes the best dress for you, and you look damn beautiful in it."

I immediately look away. I can handle Arjun being a jerk but him being a gentleman is difficult to resist. We get into the car, and after a while, we reach the walking street. The place is full of tourists like us. Arjun holds my hands tight, and I smile. He still has this protective side to him which he shows openly. And at times, it becomes borderline possessive. As we explore the place, there are so many options for food. There are stores for clothes and many artifacts. I see someone eating satay sticks. I look over the place and find the stall. I pull Arjun towards it and ask the shopkeeper to give us two portions of chicken satay. Arjun looks scared by seeing the

thing and asks, "Will it be spicy?"

"Yeah, but there is peanut butter in it which dissolves the spiciness. But it will be amazing."

I take the first bite, the spicy chicken melts in my mouth, and I make "O" with my mouth. It was hot and yummy. When I look at Arjun, I find him looking at me, and he has not eaten a single bite. "Why are you not eating? Are you one of those pretentious people who think street food is beneath their standards?" I ask to taunt him.

He smiles, "No, I eat a lot of street food, and I enjoy it too. I was watching you cause I never thought you would enjoy this kind of food after denying a fine dining and wine kind of ambiance. I would have never guessed this side of yours."

I give him a small smile, "I was not always rich and successful. And even though I have it all today, I still find happiness in enjoying the small things. People overrate materialistic things." I keep eating my satays. And I see Arjun eating them fine. I took him to a few other stalls where we tried some noodles and other items. When the time was late in the evening, we grew tired from walking and eating. I ate the whole market and Arjun enjoyed it too much. He even teased me, saying that I have a stomach of a well.

We returned to the room, and there was silence between us cause I was back to reality. I change my dress into pajama shorts and a tank top and sit quietly on the sofa. Arjun does the same. He takes out a few shot glasses and a bottle of vodka. He hands me the glasses and says, "Let's sit outside if you are not too tired eating all that junk food."

I give him an eye, and he chuckles and starts to move outside. I follow him and sit beside him.

He hands me a shot of vodka, clinks our glasses, and drinks straight up. We sit in silence. After a while, he says, "You remember we met in a similar situation in Goa. I saw you sitting like this in a dress which made you look so beautiful I couldn't even resist not coming to talk to you.

Before going on that trip, I saw you so many times in our neighborhood in Bangalore. One fine morning I saw you going to the café. You were standing in front of me in the line. You were oblivious to my presence. And after that, I saw you almost every day in the café before going to the office. Every single day you used to take your coffee, and I used to wait to get a single glance from you. I tried to know everything about you, and your journey to success is impressive. You took every step on your ladder to success with so much grace; I saw a passion in you. Not only that, as a person, you bloom like a lotus. You treat people around you with so much kindness in a world full of deceit was admirable. I became a fan of yours. Then I saw you sitting there on the beach. I knew that it was time to meet you formally. And the time we spent was like magic to my soul."

When he stopped speaking, I noticed that I was not breathing. His confession shocked me and I was unsure of how to react to the whole thing. I took one more shot, and now I was dizzy. I looked into Arjun's eyes and knew he was speaking from his heart. He was not manipulating me or anything. I was warming up to him, and it was freaking me out. Was I going to forgive him this easily?

14

Arjun- Thawing a stone

I finally took Prachi's hand and said, "Prachi, I am sorry for everything. Honestly, I am not feeling guilty for what I did, but I know you got hurt. I want you to know that I love you from the bottom of my heart, and I will move the whole world to keep you happy and safe. You are an independent woman, and I know you have everything you need in life. But I still want to provide for all your needs; I want to be the warmth that makes you sleep well at night. I want to be your safety net on which you can bounce and have fun. I want to be the air you breathe. Try to trust me and see for yourself if I am lying. I can't make this work alone."

She had tears in her eyes and was looking at the hand that I was holding. I reached to wipe her tears with my fingers and kissed her cheeks. I held her close, and she reached to me and wrapped her hands around me. I knew at that moment that I would get her back. We sat like that for a while, and then I made one more shot. I picked her up from the sand and took her into the room. We both got cleaned up and finally, we got into bed.

She was lying at the end of the bed, which made me chuckle softly. Shaking my head, I pulled her to my side.

She is so warm and feels complete in my arms. Eventually, she drifted off into sleep, and I kept looking at her again for a long time. Her face shined with the moonlight, and I felt like I had everything by my side at the moment. I know I can never let this woman leave my side, and I will protect her with everything I have in my power. Soon I had the best sleep of my life.

I opened my eyes, and rays of soft light streamed into our room. We forgot to close the blinds. I feel a heavyweight over myself, and while I look at it, I find Prachi sleeping over me. I wish to start all my mornings this way. I put her on the bed and got out. I wash up and order breakfast. I feel so good this morning; it feels too nice to be true. I go for a run, and when I return, I find Prachi sitting on the bed drinking juice. She looks so good I wish I could keep her in bed all day long with me buried deep inside her.

"Look who is finally up, Miss 'I always wake up at 5 AM." She blushed a bit.

"Well, I felt bone-tired last night, okay?" Also, I switch off my alarm. When did you wake up? Sorry, I started breakfast without you."

"It's alright! I'll wash up and join you. What do you want to do today? Want to stay on the beach or go sightseeing? We only have two more days."

"What do you mean two days? I thought we came here for a week."

Okay, so she doesn't know about my surprise plan yet. I thought Ria must have blabbed about it by now. "Well, I have planned the rest of the trip somewhere else. And it is a surprise, so make the best of your time when we are here."

"Where are we going from here? And don't tell me again it is a surprise. I want to know." God, this woman can ask me for anything, and I would give her everything. But I want to play with her while I have the chance. "Okay, I will tell you the destination, but what will I get in return?"

"What do you want?" she seems curious.

"You", I wink at her.

"What do you mean by me?" Now, her cheeks have turned red. I chuckled. "Well, when I say 'you', I mean all of you. Everything of you. The choice is yours." I gave her a coy smile. The bread toast she was chewing slides off her hand, and her mouth opens in a complete 'O'.

"You are the devil himself, aren't you? Or do you take private lessons from Lucifer himself?" She flushes her cheeks.

"Well, you can say it is an inborn talent." I say thoughtfully, scratching my beard. I laughed, "Well, let's eat breakfast first, and meanwhile, if you decide on what you want, do let me know." I winked at her again. She got flustered, and by looking at her red cheeks, I knew she was thinking about the time we spent in Goa.

I picked her up and settled her on my lap, to which she shrieked, "Wha... What are you doing?"

"What does it look like? I am feeding my wife." I took a piece of strawberry and placed it on her lips.

She took a small bite, and I took the rest and chewed it off. I take the juice glass and place it on her lips, and she takes a small sip. A few drops trickle down from the side of her lips, and I move towards her and lick them. She looks at me, breathing hard, and I feel goosebumps on her arms. I smile to realize that I still have this effect on her. I handed her a plate with an omelet and fruits on it. "Are you not going to eat?" she tried to wiggle out of my grip, but I tightened my grip on her.

"I'll eat from your plate." This is the same way I made her sit on my lap on the first morning and feed me breakfast while I was worshipping her body. She looked at me, and I kissed her forehead. “Start eating, baby; if you want to go out of this room, we need to get ready. Have you thought about what we will be doing today?”

She looked flustered....

15

Prachi- Losing it

God! What is happening right now? I should be pushing him away, but I am getting out of control with the way he is holding me and caressing my arms. His gaze is turning intense by the moment. Arjun usually has many different sides. Most of the time, he is a jerk, especially since the marriage talk started, but other times he is very gentle. And then there is this side that comes while being intimate. He becomes dominating and intense in bed, melting my panties immediately. And there is no way I can allow that to happen, but right now, all I can think of is his arms on me. This is the same way we were in Goa. He is recreating small moments that will make me forget all that has happened in these last three months.

"Maybe we can stay on the beach. We can go sightseeing tomorrow or in the evening. What do you say?" I ask him.

"Hmm... That is better. We can relax on the beach and when the sun starts to set we will visit nearby places. Come on, finish your breakfast, and we can go sooner." he shakes me slightly and chuckles when my eyes get bigger.

I finish my omelet, fill it with more, and hand him the plate. He eats and, between, keeps feeding me fruits. When he finished eating, I wiggled, trying to get out of his grasp. But he again didn't let me and said very in my ear, "Baby, if you keep wiggling your ass like that, a lot of things will start rising. And then you will be responsible for it."

I become red with embarrassment, "Arjun!" I slapped him on his arm, and he laughed, finally letting me go. I run to the bathroom close the door and wash my face. How the hell am I slipping out so easily?

Should I let go of all my inhibitions? There was a time I wanted someone in my life who could happily be with me, love me, respect me, and accept me the way I am. Isn't Arjun doing all those things right now? Ria did tell me that too.

I finally take a quick shower and come out and find Arjun lazing on the bed, keeping both his hands under his head. He looks at me, and I blush again. I look away, open my trolley, and check what I can wear. A packet in which a cotton dress was there with straps and matching bikini sets. A message on top "For a beach day." I smile. I will make it up to Sameera for organizing my bags so well. The dress is in ocean blue color. I wear it and brush my hair and make a messy bun. And apply a red matte lipstick.

I finished, and Arjun was ready too. Again he was wearing a white shirt and light blue shorts. He came near me. He took a strand of my hair over my forehead, tucked it behind my ear, and kissed my cheek, "You look stunning, baby."

"Thank you." I smile, "All credit goes to your sweet, talented sister."

He takes my hand, and we leave our cottage. We stroll around the beach, "Clothes, no clothes, you always look beautiful, Prachi. Remember that."

Okay! What do you say after something like that, does 'Thank you seem ok?

"Thank you", he smiled though I couldn't see his eyes as he wore shades. The sun was scorching, and we were strolling near the shores.

"You know this beach has an isolated part where many people don't go as they don't know about it. We can explore that if you want," he says, and I nod.

We walk through some trails and reach the end of it to find a beautiful isolated beach full of rocks. The water is crystal clear, and even the air is cooler here. It's like a paradise.

And soon, I also realize that we are completely alone here. Just the two of us in this beautiful place. In this situation, one can get scared. But one thing I know when I'm with Arjun is that he never scares me or lets anyone or anything scare me in any way.

I get rid of my dress, put it on a nearby rock, and walk into the water. Soon Arjun was with me there. He takes me deeper with him; we see coral reefs and fish inside the water. It was all so fascinating, and Arjun's presence overwhelmed me the whole time. He pulled me downward, and I gasped for air inside the water. When I came to the surface, Arjun was still holding me and laughing aloud. I slapped his chest, "God! You scared me. Why would you do that, you moron?"

He laughed again, "Come on, Prachi, live a little."

"Well, I could have drowned."

He holds me closer, and our lips touch, "I would never let you drown Prachi. Take a deep breath."

I do the same, and he asks me to hold my breath and pulls us underwater. I look around, and everything is mesmerizing.

When we come to the surface again, I hold on to him for my dear life. At that moment, I get the urge to kiss him, and

I brush my lips on his. He stills for a few seconds, and I pull away.

We look into each other's eyes while he grasps my neck and brings my lips to his, and I melt away. I remember how good it was to kiss this beautiful man. The passion, the intensity, and the fire all come at once. I forget everything in the world, and one thing remains for us! Our body molds together within the water, and we kiss like no tomorrow. Our tongues meddled with each other, and our hands roamed over each other's bodies. It's like breathing fresh air.

When we finally move apart, we both are breathing hard. Arjun has this look of hunger in his eyes, and his jaw ticks again. So he ticks his jaw when he gets horny, well, that's interesting.

He takes me near a rock while being inside the water and removes my bikini. He moves me closer, kisses me behind my ears, and bites my earlobes, and I stop breathing. My body starts warming, and all the hotness starts moving between my legs.

He slowly pinches my nipples, and a moan escapes my lips. He starts squeezing my breasts, giving each one equal attention same time, kissing me all over. The water keeps swishing against our bodies, and it has a weird effect. The sun shining and reflecting over Arjun's body makes him look invincible. God, how did this happen? He is the type of handsome guy who breaks hearts, and somehow, I find myself on the path to being one of them. The only thing is will I be able to retake a heartbreak?

I clung to him while his fingers started moving south. Automatically my hand moves over his abs, his beautiful, well-defined abs, which he has been showcasing to me for the last couple of days shamelessly. I hover over his swimming trunks and feel him over the fabric. He is rock-hard; I forgot how big and thick he is. It has been over a year since I had a feel for him. He slides his fingers over my bikini bottoms over my clit. I moan loudly. “Yes, baby, moan for me,” he says, and I remember how dirty he talks.

16

Arjun- Finally in my arms

She feels so good in my arms. It surprised me when she initiated the kiss, but I lost all my control the moment she kissed me. I slide a finger into her wet folds, and she moans, and that's the music I need all day long. Her moans always make me feel alive. I slide another finger much deeper this time, and damn, she feels tight.

I scissor my fingers inside her, and she moans louder while coming on my fingers. If we weren't in the water, I would have licked her clean and made her orgasm a couple more times. But right now, I want to be deep inside her.

Once she comes from the shock of her orgasm, she slides her hand inside my swimming trunks and starts rubbing my cock real hard as if she can't get enough of it. Before I lose myself completely, I stop her midway. I position her legs around my hips after sliding my shorts down. I rub my cock on her clit to tease her, "Arjun, please, I need you." And I take that as my cue, and I slide inside her, and she lets a scream out. She feels so tight I am going to come in a few seconds. I start moving while kissing her luscious lips; she moans the whole time. I started fucking her hard and fast without letting her breathe, and she came, biting my lower lip. I bite her nipples to keep the fire in her alive and give deeper strokes. “Come for me, baby.” I was like some drug addict who was tasting his favorite drug after coming from rehab. And with her moans reaching for the climax, I come with her.

We both lose our balance, but I hold her tight so she doesn’t sink into the water. I kiss her lips again, “How dare you keep what’s mine away from me for so long, sweetheart? You are going to pay for this, you know.”

“W... What?” She looks at me with confusion written on her face. I pull her out of the water and help her put on her bikini top. I take her dress off the rock, put it on her, and wear my clothes as well. I kiss her forehead, and she looks at me with doe eyes. I take her hand and start to move towards the path back to our cottage. I can’t believe I took her like that inside the water the first time after our marriage. This was not how I planned our first sex post-marriage. But I will make it up to her. She is reticent. I peek at her, and she is looking down the whole time. “Prachi, are you alright? Did I hurt you?” This woman will make me a moose.

She looks up at me and bites her lip. Oh, that lip! “I am good,” She says, but her face is telling me that she is lying. So I stopped walking and held her face so she would look into my eyes and ask again, “Are you ok, Prachi? Is something bothering you? Or maybe you regret what just happened?”

She blushes again, and her face becomes red, “No, really, I am good. And I don’t regret what happened at all. I was just wondering and thinking about something.”

Hmm... that swells my heart, but what is she wondering that makes her blush like that? Prachi is not like those shy, sweet women kind. She is tough, stronger, and doesn't give a fuck about anything type of person. So seeing her blush this way is new for me.

I start walking again, holding her hands, "What are you wondering about?"

She looks away, and I bring her face towards me so she can talk to me, "I was just wondering if you dated someone else after I left Goa." She is still avoiding looking at me. And I laughed at the thought. How can she even wonder something like that? I have not even looked at someone other than her in three years. "I am sorry to disappoint you, sweetheart, but I was too busy to get you back into my life for dating someone else. And if you are wondering if I had sex with someone else after you, then the answer is no. After having a feel of a fine woman like you, everything else feels tasteless."

Now she looks into my eyes and releases a sigh of contentment, I guess, so I ask again, "And what were you thinking about?"

I am always curious to know more about her. "I never thought that if we ever had sex again, it would be so beautiful and unique." she smiles slowly.

I look at her with surprise; how does this woman always find new ways to surprise me, "You think that was beautiful and unique?"

"Don't you? The water, beautiful view, open sky, isolated island. It's like living a movie tale or something." she gives a beautiful smile. Haa! She is the most down-to-earth girl. She is not like another woman who always demands to have luxury. Prachi takes life easy and enjoys small and natural things.

I smile at that thought when she asks, "Why are we leaving this beautiful island?"

Because we didn't bring any food with us, playing in the water for so long will make both of us tired soon." We can come later again. But I want you in our cottage on our bed right now." I give her a naughty smile. She gives me a smirk, and I know I have my woman back. But I also liked her girly side.

Once we reach our cottage, I take her to the bathroom and draw a bath for both of us. And once we are in the bathtub, I hold her to me and kiss her the hell of it. Her desperation meets mine, and I push two fingers deep inside her. She squirms in my arms, and I bite her lip to contain her excitement. She is feisty like I remember, and I enjoy controlling her emotions. I take her to the edge and pull out my fingers. She begs me, "Arjun pleaseeee!"

I take her nipples into my mouth and bite them hard till she screams my name. I pinch the other nipple, and she scratches my back with her nails which gets me roaring. I push three fingers inside her, and she comes screaming my name. And I let her cling to me like she is going to die. She overcomes the shock of orgasm and kisses me again like she is reaching for oxygen.

I swipe her out of the tub, wrap her in a fresh towel, and dry myself with another one. I take her to the bed and claim her lips, and she wraps her arms around my neck. Her skin is so soft and smooth that I want to bite her and mark her all over. I move towards her neck and keep going down between her boobs, kissing, biting, and licking all the time. I brush my hand over her inner thigh and squeeze lightly, and she yelps.

I smile, enjoying her moans and screams. I grab her legs and position them over my shoulders.

She closes her eyes in anticipation, and I don't like her hiding those emotions from me, "Open your eyes and look at me, babe. Never close your eyes. Watch me while I give you all the pleasures."

Her eyes get bigger as I move towards her sensitive core. I start licking her clit, and she pleads with me for more. I push two fingers inside her and put my thumb on her clit, giving a good amount of pressure while biting her nipples. She comes, and I lap around her core.

"You taste just as I remember, sweetheart."

"Arjun, please, I can't wait anymore," she pleads.

"What do you want, baby?" I smirk at her.

"I need you inside me right now," she growls at me, and I smile. This is what I was missing, the fire and need in her to command me this way.

"Your wish is my command, my lady." I make the gesture of making a bow in front of her and pushing inside her in one stroke.

17

Prachi- On fire

My whole body is on fire. Each touch of his is melting me from inside, becoming a pool of nerves. Even when he is deep inside me, he gives attention to my whole body. He keeps kissing me on the lips, biting and licking my neck, pinching, and sucking my nipples. I have already lost control of myself, and he keeps moving in and out of my body. After a while, I come, and my whole body shudders, and after a few more strokes, he comes inside me and lies on me.

We both breathe hard, trying to calm ourselves. He moves off me, and I miss his weight over my body. He looks at me for a few seconds, "Are you ok? You look a bit flushed. Was I too rough?"

Yeah, but I loved every second of it. Though having sex with Arjun is always intense, today, I felt a bit of pent-up aggression in him. As if he had been waiting for this moment for a long time. I smile at him, "I am good. I am more than good, and no, you were not too rough. You were perfect." I look away, and he brings my face to look at him and kisses my lips. He gets out of bed, washes in the bathroom, and brings a wet towel. He cleans me up very gently. He pulls me into his lap, and I remember him saying something at the beach today. "Hey, what were you saying at the beach today about me keeping something of yours away from you for such a long time? I got distracted and forgot about it."

He moves his hand all over my body and licks my lips, "This, you, you are mine, everything about you is mine. And you kept yourself away from me and left me. You have no idea how painful it was when you left me in Goa like that. And then every week, I had to watch you from far away going on day in and day out. From the moment I kissed you in Goa, you were mine. And honestly, I am still angry with you for leaving me like that." His eyes are glowing. The nerve of this man. He is angry! After turning my world upside down in these past months, he is angry with me!

"You are angry? Oh! Yeah, you are angry cause you have not made my life a useless mess. You have made me a person who doesn't have any control over her life. And yet you are angry, right!" I realize I am screaming at him, and still, his arms are around me. I feel his hardness near my ass.

"God! This is turning you on? What kind of a creep are you?"

"Only for you, baby." He gives me a wide beautiful smile. He flips me over the bed and hovers over me, pinning my hands over my head.

"Yes, baby, I turned your life upside down. I made you lose control, and I will do it again if you ever even think about leaving me. Losing you at that time was unbearable, and I will make sure you never do that in this lifetime. And you are not getting out of this bed till we leave this place."

He claims my lips again while I ponder over his words. He is finally showing his possessiveness when it should make me mad; it makes me feel warm all over my heart.

After feeding me a good amount of food, he retakes me. After around round three, I slump into his arms feeling completely exhausted. We both sleep like logs till the sun starts to stream through the curtains. I open my eyes and find myself lying over Arjun. I don't know how I always end up sleeping all over him every night since the day we got married. He looks even more beautiful sleeping like this. I study his chest and abdomen area. Wait! Does he have a tattoo?

How did I miss this? It is quite small and over his shoulder. I have always focused on his abs to notice this, but I do remember that he didn't have this last year. Did he get this recently?

It is an anchor surrounded by thorn wire surrounding it but the wire breaks at one end. What does it mean?

I look at his face, and I get a warmth within my chest. How have I reached a point of having these kinds of feelings for him in just a couple of days of being with him? Since I have already let him into my boundaries, will I be able to handle it when everything goes south? Will he, too,

break my heart at one point? I know he is capable of doing that.

I slip out of bed, run to the bathroom, get cleaned up, brush my teeth, and take a cold shower. I wear a tank top and shorts, brush my hair and make a pony. After getting ready, I find Arjun still sleeping peacefully. I smile at that and get out of the cottage towards the ocean. I walk along the shore while being deep in my thoughts.

I realize I know nothing about Arjun's past. Was he ever in a relationship

with anyone? My parents seem to adore him; he has won their hearts in a beat. He has charmed my best friend Ria too. She thinks he is a great guy to spend the rest of my life with.

Though his family is awesome, today is our last day in Thailand, and tomorrow we will go to another place. He has kept it secret for God knows what reason.

I found a small café near the shore. I get inside and get two coffees to go along with some sandwiches. I return to the cottage and find Arjun talking to someone over the phone. His tone is bossy and stressed. I guess it is work-related, and I slide silently into the room. He looks at me and gives me a blazing smile. I smile at him and hand him his coffee. He ends his call, takes the coffee and breakfast from my hands, and puts it on the side table. And then he picks me up in his arms, jumps on the bed, and kisses me. I giggle at that. He turns me around and spanks my ass lightly, "Why did you leave me alone in bed? I wanted to devour you first thing in the morning."

"Shut up, you moron! I am sore from last night and drink your coffee, or it will get cold."

He kisses my forehead and takes his coffee. We had our breakfast sitting outside our cottage. The whole day Arjun made me forget that a world outside exists. We spent the entire day inside the cottage and the whole evening on the beach talking and playing in the water. By the end of it, I was more than exhausted. But the day went swimmingly, as we got to talk a lot.

By the time it was the evening, we had returned to our cottage after having a light dinner. My curiosity was getting the best of me by now, "At what time are we leaving tomorrow? I get to know that, at least right?"

He gives me a laugh, "Of course, sweetheart! I know you contain your curiosity to the best, but it will be worth it, believe me on that. And we will be leaving early morning tomorrow. It will be a whole day flight to our next destination."

"A whole day? Do you mean 24 hours? Are you crazy?"

"Yup! I know it will be tiring, but you will be happy when you reach there."

"Oh, come on! Tell me where we are going now." I am getting irritated now.

"Prachi, as you have waited so long, you can wait a little longer. Plus, I will entertain you the entire time. I promise you that. After all, there are perks of traveling in a private jet." he wiggles his eyebrows at me, and I huff in reaction.

18

Prachi- Falling for him

The next day we checked out of our stay at 7 AM, and I sighed, thinking of traveling again for so long. But I was also looking forward to whatever Arjun had planned for the rest of the honeymoon. Even though I didn't want to come on this trip with Arjun, he wooed me as expected. My self-restraint is much, much weaker than I thought.

And as promised, Arjun kept me busy throughout the flight time, and being so exhausted; I slept half of it in his arms like a log. Finally, Arjun woke me up, "Wake up, sleepy head. We will be landing in an hour, and if you sleep anymore, you won't be able to sleep at night."

He was kissing and biting near my earlobe and neck. I kissed him on his lips. I freshened up and changed into shorts and a T-shirt Arjun kept on the bed for me. Once I was ready, I sat with Arjun, and we were both quiet. He was caressing my arm.

I get an urge to ask and break the ice, "Were you ever in a long-term relationship?"

He looks at me with surprised eyes. Is it because I asked such a question out of nowhere? But I have wanted to ask this for a long time now.

"Yes, I was in a long-term relationship once."

That got my complete attention, "What happened?"

"Hmm... Well, I was out of college and was working in one of the real estate companies. Before joining my father's business, I was trying to learn and gain experience. My father, at that time, owned a small construction company; my vision was to expand and grow it. I met Archana there. She was a PA to one of the company's higher management personnel. She was as beautiful and smart as a fox. We were together for almost five years. After completing four years in the company, I resigned to join my father. We even started living together. On her birthday I thought of surprising her in her office. I went with flowers, and a cake and I also brought a ring to propose to her. I had friends in the office, so I got an easy pass into her office without her knowing. But when I reached there, I found her fucking her boss. The view shattered my mind. I left the place before we could even talk. The same evening, I got a call from the hospital saying Archana had an accident. I was her emergency contact as we were staying together. I went to the hospital to see her, but she was in a very critical condition. She was in surgery the whole night, but they told me she couldn't survive it the next morning."

I was shivering, and my whole body went cold, "She died?" To which he nodded.

God! What must that be like? And here I thought I had a bad past. He seems so cool all the time. But deep down, he has a ghost lurking behind his neck. I hold his hand, "I am so sorry for everything you went through. I don't know how you went past it, but you are so strong, Arjun. And you are very brave and mature as the person that you are today."

I don't know why but tears start rolling down my cheeks, and everything becomes blurry. He wipes my cheeks with his thumb, "Prachi, it was 7 years ago. It was devastating, but I knew it was not my fault. And I found out later that she was cheating on me from the beginning of our relationship. Her accident opened my eyes in a true sense. Life is very short, and living in pain will only make it shorter. That was the day I promised myself I would live my life on my terms and be happy. And anytime I want something, I grab it and take it with me."

"Just like you did with me?" I ask.

"Yes, Prachi. Just like I did with you. After Archana, I never thought I would meet someone I could trust and love so much, but then you came into my life. I knew I could let you go, and who knows what will happen the next moment? So I made my life goal to get you back into my life." his eyes are shining with pride. If he is like this in life, I want to see him in action when he handles work.

"Enough about me, sweetheart. We are about to land. Be ready for your surprise." he gives me a wicked grin, and I grab him by the nape and kiss him till I take all his hidden pain with me.

Once we land, my jaw drops to the floor. He brought me to Miami. Fucking Miami! I can't blink my eyelids cause I feel like it will all vanish, and I will wake up from a dream in my house. I look at him, and he is smiling. Is he for real? He takes my hand in his, walks me through the airport, and we get into a cab. The whole city is so damn bright and sparkly that it hurts my eyes.

When we reached our stay, I saw a big villa again in front of the beach. The whole place is bustling with people. "Is this someone's house?" I ask.

"Yeah, it is one of my friend's villas. Let's get inside. I have some more jaw-dropping moments for you." he said, pulling me along with him.

When we enter the villa, candles, and fairy lights fill the whole place. I look at the place with awe and go inside, “Your friend let you stay here for our honeymoon?”

“Yes. But this is not all.” he stands behind me and wraps his arms around me. “There is one more surprise for you.”

“What more can there be?”

And that’s when everyone comes screaming toward me, and in a blur, I see Ria, Sameera, and Rahul in front of me. Ria hugs me in a tight hold, and my mind starts spinning, wondering, “What is happening? How are you guys here?”

I look at Arjun, standing behind me and smiling politely. I go to him, and again he holds me in his arms, “You called them here?”

He looks into my eyes and ponders for a while, "Actually, I was worried that you would not be happy with our trip." So I thought if they were here, you would be able to enjoy it more, but honestly, I am regretting it now.” I laugh at his response. It was so thoughtful of him; he wanted me to enjoy this trip even though he was sad about it; he asked all my people to come. And most of them are his siblings. He didn’t expect me to forgive him so easily. He whispers in my ears, “I just want to take you to our room and fuck you till we both lose our senses.” And I get tingles all over my body.

At the same time, a guy enters the hall; he is tall, rugged, and very good-looking. Who is this? Is he Arjun’s friend who owns this villa? As if noticing my questionable look, Arjun introduced me, “Prachi, this is my best friend in the world, Avisek. And Avisek meet my wife Prachi.” Being introduced as a wife feels weird. But I extend my hand to shake Avisek’s and say, "It is nice to meet you." I notice Sameera getting tensed by the minute. Fascinating, so some stories are there to uncover. The writer in me is always looking for new stories.

Ria takes me away and hugs me again. "How are you? And you look so tan. Did you spend the whole three days on the beach?"

"Yeah, kind of. How are you? And Sameera, how are you? I liked all my dresses; they are great," they both giggle and smile at me.

"We are good, but we missed you. So how have these last three days been for you? You are glowing, and the way you and Bhai entered here didn't look like you were angry with him anymore," Sameera asks.

I smile shyly, "Well, things happened, and your brother is a charmer, and that's all you are gonna get from me." They both giggle again louder.

Arjun stands with Rahul and Avisek, and our eyes meet. Standing so far, and yet he has this effect on me.

19

Arjun- Worth it!

I look at my beautiful wife from across the room talking with the girls, and she seizes my heart. I planned this for her so that she could enjoy this place with her friends even in my presence.

Even though I regret it right now, as I see her smile, everything seems worth it.

Rahul finally takes my attention, "So how are things going with Prachi? She is smiling for a change."

"Everything is going good."

"How did this happen in just three days? Last I saw, she looked at you with all the hate in the world."

I smile, "I don't know, but I tried to be honest with her this time. We had too much time to be alone with each other, and I wanted her to see my side of emotions. She somehow decided to give us a chance, I guess."

"I am happy for you, Bhai. You deserve to be happy. And I can say Prachi is the best woman for you," I know Rahul means that for me.

"Well, it's time I go to my wife. Let's meet tomorrow morning.", I say, and I move towards Prachi.

All three girls are laughing and giggling, and I wrap myself around the one taking my breath away. I kiss her forehead, "It's late now, baby. Wanna you get some sleep? Tomorrow you can have all the fun again." I smile at her, and she smiles back and nods. Sameera smiles, and Ria gives me a small nod in agreement.

I hold her hand and take her with me towards our room. The moment we enter, I take my wife in my arms and kiss her. "So, did you like the surprise? Are you happy?"

"Yes, I am happy, and I love your surprise. But promise me on our next trip, it will be just us alone," she giggles. God, this is my second favorite sound in the world. I take her to the bathroom and fuck her in the shower to hear her moan and giggle. It was the first thing I noticed about her in Goa. She giggles while I worship her body. Usually, women are very intense during sex or fake to be intense. Still, Prachi always enjoys it to the fullest, like me.

I bring her back to our bed and gently put her on it. She has already started to doze off due to exhaustion. I slide beside her and hold her in my arms. My life has taken a new leaf in a couple of days. And now that she has begun to accept me in her life, my feelings for her are getting much

deeper. She asked me about my past, and I shared it with her. But the truth is, even for Archana, I never felt like this. The obsession, the possessiveness, the protectiveness, and the urge to be inside her all the fucking time. How can someone make you feel like that? Will she ever be able to see how much I need her in my life?

She molds her body with mine in sleep, and I fall into an abyss.

I wake up and find Prachi sleeping peacefully. I checked the time, and it was 5 in the morning. I guess I am catching on to my wife's schedule. I want to take Prachi to the beach because I know she will enjoy the cool air now. I slowly slip out of her grasp and move towards her legs. I spread her and start lapping at her core, and she moans even when she is asleep. I smile at the thought of waking her up every morning like this. I push a finger inside her, keep licking her clit, and she lazily opens her eyes. Unable to understand what is happening, she sits with a jolt, "Arjun!"

"Yes, baby, you like your new morning alarm?" I ask, raising my eyebrows.

"God! You are a sex manic, aren't you?" She asks with a smile. I get to eat her pussy again, and she falls back on the bed and starts squirming and screaming. When she comes, I don't give her time to come back to life and push my cock inside her in one go. She stops breathing due to the intrusion, and I start moving inside her. We both fall into each other's arms after we climax. I know I don't want to miss the sunrise, so I take her to the bathroom and wash us both.

We spent the morning watching the sunrise and playing in the water. The days go by as others join us after a while.

20

Prachi- Changes with anxiety

We are back from our honeymoon today, and I am reminiscing all the small to big moments I spent with Arjun. I can't believe I hated him with all my energy a week back, and now I don't want to be apart from him even for a while.

For a change, I am looking forward to starting my new life with my husband. Well, that adds a ring to it I haven't gotten used to yet.

Since coming home, I have been working in my home office and spending time with my new family and my parents. Days are going in a blur. I am looking at the screen of my laptop, and yet my mind is remembering the time in the morning when Arjun woke me up at 5 AM, saying it was happy hours. He has a habit now of waking me up every day, either having his head between my legs or while being inside me. And he doesn't let me get out of bed until I have to beg him for it. I am living in a happy bubble and am scared it will burst at any point. Honestly, I am still not over the fact that Arjun manipulated me into this marriage. But

I think I wouldn't have agreed to be with him anytime soon. Ria is working in Bangalore this week, and I am missing her right now.

We have never been apart since we started our company. But she said some of our clients wanted to have meetings sooner on the contracts that she is handling. I wanted to stay with her in the office, but she forced me to be back in Jabalpur, being newly married and all. Since she is always with me, she helps me focus on work without losing my mind to different thoughts.

But I have caught something between her and Rahul. They both have been giving this vibe that I am not sure is casual or something serious. They hang out together a lot, but Ria has never mentioned anything to me. I thought she shared everything with me. But since I am very private,

I don't like stepping into someone else's boundaries. Whatever it is, I hope everything works out for both of them. I don't want any of them to get hurt in the path they are taking.

Sameera and Avisek have a different thing going on. In Miami, I asked Sameera about Avisek and she informed me that things are complicated. It seems Sameera had a crush on him since she was a teenager. She confessed the same to Avisek when she was 16 years old. Since Avisek is 6 years older than her, he rejects her on the spot, saying she is a kid and Arjun's baby sister.

Which is I think Avisek did the right thing at that age. But I also saw Avisek looking at Sameera with an intense gaze. So there is some other story involved.

I focus myself back on work, and after a few hours, I go down to the hall to be with my parents.

They are both quite calm these days. I talked with them for some time while drinking coffee.

I go back to my office and down myself with my huge workload. I lose track of time while working, and that is why I need Ria with me all the time.

I called Ria to discuss our new projects and new contracts in the market that we can bid for. We go on for hours. I was already exhausted, but work piled up since I was not working for the whole two weeks...

21

Arjun- Finding peace

It has been a hectic day with me traveling for a new project. We have a new project of setting up a plant in Barela, and I had to leave early this morning. We visited the plant site to discuss the construction details. And I haven't talked with Prachi since the morning after we had breakfast together with the family. I thought of calling her, but I have been busy with the blast of unread emails in my inbox.

When I reach home, my mother comes out of Prachi's house into our gates. I kiss her on the cheeks and smile at her. "It is just two weeks to your marriage, and both of you have immersed yourself in work again, I see.", my mother comments. I laugh at that, "Mom, we both run our companies; it is not easy to leave work as it is. Plus, Rahul has been handling all the work on my behalf for the past two weeks, and I guess Ria was doing the same for Prachi. They can't go on like that for us to sit peacefully, or both of them will go mad."

"Yeah, I know. Prachi has been working since morning too. She didn't even have lunch, as her mother said."

"Is she working from her home office?" I ask. To which my mother nods. My mother is the calmest person I know.

She is even calm and collected in stressful situations and has always taught me to stay the same in life. I have inherited this trait from her, I guess, whereas everything else, I am exactly like my father.

I see my father reading a book on the lawn. He is enjoying his retired life pretty well. I am happy to see him relaxed after working so hard throughout his life. I sit with both of them with a cup of coffee. Usually, these days they spend the most time with Prachi's parents. They are even planning a trip with them, and it fills me with gratitude.

My mom asks me something, and since I zoned out for a while, she laughs and repeats her question, "Do you know what is going on with Rahul these days? He seems happy, but he rarely shares anything with us. I have seen him talking with Ria sometimes."

I laugh at her nosy comment, "Mom, let him be. If he is happy, everything will work out in the way they want. I have seen them hang out often, and they bond well, but he hasn't shared much with me either."

Mom seems thoughtful for a while, "Ria is a nice girl. If they like each other, then I hope they work on it soon. I want another daughter-in-law." I smile at her knowing she wants our family to grow. I see Rahul come into the lawn area, and I laugh, knowing very well what awaits him.

As expected, my mother takes charge of her plans, "Rahul, are you not dating anyone?"

Rahul is a bird who doesn't like to sit on a tree and make his nest there. He likes to fly from one tree to another and enjoy his freedom, so this will be interesting.

"Oh, Come on, Mom! I am young and having fun right now. Bhai got married. So let him and Prachi have the spotlight for now. I am nowhere near to settling down right now."

My father huffs and goes back to his book. Rahul looks shocked that our father is quietly making disgruntled noises. Mom says, "I know you are enjoying your life. But I am saying that if you ever feel like a girl is important to you, don't ignore that feeling for the sake of your so-called freedom."

And for the first time, I see Rahul as thoughtful and quiet. I stand up from my chair and wish them good night. I miss my woman, and I need to see her now. I freshen up, wear my tracksuit pants and a plain T-shirt, and go towards Prachi's house. The moment I entered their hall, I saw my father-in-law sitting and watching some videos on his phone. And my mother-in-law is sitting beside him, dozing off. I smile seeing them together like this. The moment they see me, a smile appears on their faces. Prachi's parents are the most decent and simple people I have ever met.

I guess that's the reason Prachi is so amazing.

Her mom asks me if I had dinner, to which I deny. "Even Prachi hasn't eaten anything yet. Since morning she has been having meetings and working non-stop. Let me get something to eat for both of you. Maybe you can make her stop working and eat the damn food." I laugh at her motherly irritation.

"I guess Prachi has been a handful to raise," I comment. She shakes her head and laughs, saying, "You have no idea. She was a notorious kid. Most of the time, she was lonely, but she used to play on her own, which attracted a lot of accidents and getting injured."

I give her a shocked face, and she continues to explain, "You see, she had a temper issue from childhood and used to get irritated with everything. And her fun time was climbing trees or jumping off some wall. Most of the evening, she used to ride her bicycle around the street and came home bleeding. I was always anxious about her whereabouts."

I laughed, knowing Prachi kept her parents on their toes throughout her childhood. My father-in-law came from behind while keeping his hands on my shoulders; he said, "Now she will keep you on your toes. She is grown up now, but don't think her nature has changed much."

I smile at both of them, saying I will take good care of her. And they nod. I take the plates of food with me to Prachi's office.

22

Arjun- So pure and naive!

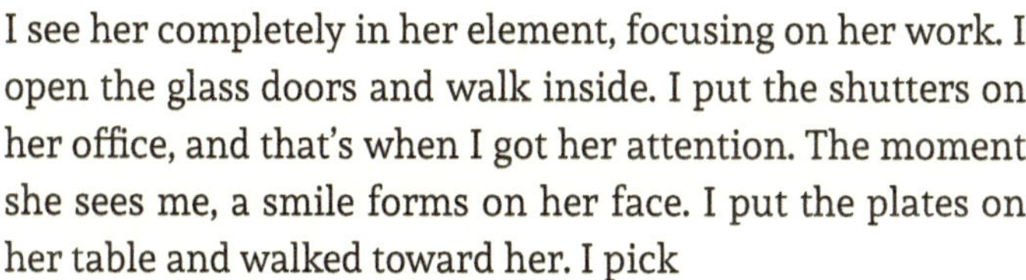

I see her completely in her element, focusing on her work. I open the glass doors and walk inside. I put the shutters on her office, and that's when I got her attention. The moment she sees me, a smile forms on her face. I put the plates on her table and walked toward her. I pick

her up from the chair, take her place, and make her sit on my lap. She squeals in response.

"When did you come back? How was your day?" She fires questions at me.

"I came back an hour ago. I was spending time with our parents knowing you were busy. My day was tiring, and I missed you a lot."

She chuckles, "I missed you too."

"Liar! You have been enjoying working your ass off. That's why you didn't even have lunch.", I accuse her playfully.

She makes a pout face, "Did my mother rat me out? I swear she is trying to make me fat. I ate some fruit and was not feeling hungry. And yes, I was enjoying my work, but I still missed you. I kept thinking about you and had to work this long because of it."

She is so damn cute when she wants to be, "Is your work done?"

"It is for now. I can continue later." She gives me a mouth-watering kiss.

I want to be inside her this instant, but I know she hasn't eaten the whole day. So I better control myself. I take the plates and hand them to her to hold. I never thought I would enjoy feeding someone and making them sit on my lap. Also, I noticed she always eats her food without any complaints. She is not very picky about food and enjoys eating everything. Most women make a lot of diet and fuss about fat and carbs in their food.

After we finished dinner, I took her to her room. And this is the first time I am in her room. It is clean and well-organized. I am scared to mess something in here. Books stack one whole wall. And all the books look super clean. She has hardcover binders for all classic novels. I knew she was a nerd, but this is another level of nerd. I guess that explains how she established such a successful company in a short period. Plus, I have observed Ria, and she seems to be some kind of genius.

While I go through her book collection, Prachi wraps her arms around my back and says, "Don't even think about stealing even a single book. You can borrow it but have to return it. This my biggest asset."

She seems proud of herself and smiles like a small baby showcasing her favorite toys in mint condition. I guess it is true what they say, 'Silent type people are the wildest and naughtiest people in this world.'

I tease her, "Don't worry, Ma'am. I will never even touch your precious books without your permission. Now, will I get a reward for being good?"

She laughs and then gives me a sexy smile, "What do you want as a reward?"

"If you have to ask the question, then I guess I haven't made myself clear before this moment." I flip her on my shoulder and take her to the bathroom. I undress her and myself. I enter the shower holding her in my arms, and I move her around, push towards the shower wall, and bite her neck. I move my hand over her firm ass. I spank her lightly first, and she gasps in reaction.

"All I ever want is you, baby. I want to imprint it in your smart brain."

I spank her a few more times with increasing intensity than before. Then I separate her legs by moving my thigh between hers. I find her dripping wet when I move my fingers over her folds.

"Look what we have here. My baby likes being spanked, is it? Who are you this wet for, baby?"

In response, she only whimpers, and I spank her again, "Answer me, sweetheart."

She moans again and finally replies, "For you, you moron. Now, fuck me already. I have been waiting all day to have you inside me." I smile wickedly and push three fingers inside her while rubbing her clit with my thumb. She orgasms in a few pumps, and I push my cock deep inside her. And I show her how much I need her.

We lie down on the bed, and while she is in my arms, I make her lie on my chest. I caress her cheeks, "Can I ask something?"

She looks me in the eyes, "Sure. Anything."

I think about how to frame my question. Because when I want her to be open with me, I don't want to make her feel uncomfortable, "I know you had a boyfriend from college.

My parents told me it was bad the way you guys broke up. What happened?"

She goes quiet for some time, and if I made a mistake by asking this. But she moves away from me and sits, crossing her legs and facing me. I also move to sit, keeping my head supported on the headrest. She plays with her fingers and looks toward the glass wall.

"His name was Madhav. I met him during my first year of college days. And we instantly clicked. We started dating. All was good till college ended. I got a job in a graphics design start-up. And, they paid me well. He was struggling in the initial days but eventually got a job in an architectural firm. We decided to move in together. After a year, he said we should buy a house. During my college days, I used to do freelance work from which I made huge savings. He knew that I was saving to start my own company one day. But somehow, he convinced me of our future together and how buying a house at an earlier age would be better for us. I agreed, and we bought the apartment in Bangalore by paying all my savings as a down payment. We were paying EMI monthly, but even that was not 50-50. He used to say he was supporting his family, and I urged him that I would pay most of the EMI. I loved him. And when you stay with a person for so long, you start to weave dreams around them. In my college days, Madhav and I spent

most of our time in my dorm room. My roommate Shristi was my best friend at that time. And, Madhav and Shristi also became good friends. After college, Shristi used to come to our house to spend time with Madhav and me. I was happy that they were getting along so well cause Shristi was my only friend. Sometimes when I used came from the office, I used to find them together watching movies or playing games. And I am not a person who gets suspicious easily. I was too focused on my career and plans. One time I came to visit my parents for a week. While going back, there was a cancellation on my flight, so I booked the ticket for a day early. I thought I would surprise Madhav, and he will be happy."

I listen to her narration without interrupting her, but my blood is boiling inside. I knew the gist, but I guess she didn't tell anyone the full story. And while she is telling me all, in my head, I am planning the devastation of the guy who broke the love of my life. I would give my life to the woman who is so precious to me and might take some as well. But I want her to finish her story.

I already know what happened afterward, but it's better if she gets it all out of her chest. She becomes silent for a while. Her eyes are shining with tears, which is killing me right now.

"When I reached my apartment and unlocked it with my key, I was expecting him to be in his office. I planned to decorate the whole apartment and make a special dinner for him. But my excitement was short-lived. As I entered the hall, I heard noises coming from our bedroom. My heart was beating so loud that I felt like I might lose myself at that moment. I moved towards the bedroom without making any noise. As I slowly opened the door, I saw Madhav and Shristi having sex on our bed. The whole scene was unimaginable. When they noticed me, they weren't surprised. Shristi groaned and huffed as if I ruined her fun time while Madhav was breathing hard and looked mad. I waited for them to wear their clothes. Once done, Madhav's reaction was shocking to me. He said he was glad I finally found out. Shristi said that I should accept everything as it is and leave Madhav's life. I was angry at this point because

I didn't know what to do or where to go. Shristi also mentioned that they had been having an affair since college and loved each other. When I asked Madhav for an explanation for his betrayal, he said that Shristi was better than me in bed. And she knew how to please a man. We got into a fight, and Shristi slapped me. When I charged toward her, Madhav stopped my tracks and threw me to the floor. He asked me to leave our house, and when I asked why I should leave, he told me that I couldn't do anything about it. That made sense; I was suffocating there. So I packed important stuff and left. We had a joint account for savings for our future. He cleaned it all in a few hours."

"I went to a hotel for a few days. I wanted to clear my head with everything that happened to me. Then I remembered it all. All the flights Madhav and I had. Every time I dressed, Madhav commented about how I should dress like a girl, how I should maintain myself, and be more appealing. He used to comment on my skills in bed as well. But I never took it very seriously because he always used to say it playfully. It was a good thing I had some emergency savings. So I searched for a shared apartment and moved on with my life. I found Ria there, and then the rest is history."

I am shocked to the core. I know the pain of betrayal, but mental abuse and manipulation are different. Now I understand why she never considered the idea of giving us a chance. And I was right; she would have never given me an opportunity. And my manipulating her to marry me is something that must have caused her an equal amount of pain.

23

Prachi- The revelation

I watch Arjun's face and see anger and pain in his eyes. I know what he is thinking. He is thinking about how we got married and now he knows how much pain he has caused me. But other than that, I see anger to a level I never thought Arjun was capable of having. He is always calm and collected. This is the first time I can visibly see him enraged.

He takes my hand in his and pulls me to his chest. He wraps his arms around me. I spill tears instantly. He is shaking and keeps caressing my back.

"Prachi, I am so sorry. So sorry for giving you so much pain and making you go through everything with this marriage. I know you may not forgive me, but I will spend my whole life making it up to you. And that bastard will pay for everything he did to you. For everything they did to you." his words slice me from inside and heal the wound that has been inside me for the past four years.

"I am okay now. I don't bother much about what happened." I tell him. I don't like it when people fuss over me.

"You can lie to the whole world, baby but not me. I have been observing you for more than three years. The first time I saw you, you were standing in front of me in the queue in the café in front of our apartments. You had your headphones on and hardly even looked at anyone. Something about you caught my attention. I knew the look on your face pretty well. It was the same I used to give to the world. You were trying to say to the world, 'Fuck you all. You don't deserve my time or attention.' And You looked beautiful. You were sanitizing your hands obsessively." He pauses for a minute, and I listen to him with an open mouth.

"I saw pain and aggression on your face, which comes off as arrogance to the world. The next day I saw you again in the café leaving with your coffee. After that, it became a habit for me to go early to the café. I used to sit with my coffee and wait for you to come. Every day, I hoped that you would look at me once, but that never happened. When I saw you sitting on the beach, lost in your thoughts, I couldn't resist. I just wanted to talk to you. But when we kissed the first time, I knew you were an obsession for me that I wanted to turn into a possession. I know you are not an object I can have as a possession, but I couldn't stop myself until we got married. Believe me, Prachi, you mean everything to me, and I couldn't think of any other way you would have stayed with me. So I did what I had to. But now I understand my actions only increased your pain, and I am extremely sorry for that."

Tears are spilling from my eyes as if I have opened a dam gate of a reservoir inside me. He pulled me to him, licked my tears, and kissed my forehead. He looks deep in thought and asks, "What about the apartment you bought together?"

I look away from him, not knowing how to reply, "They both are still staying there together." It is the most humiliating thing, and I have never told anyone this many details.

He gasps, "What? Why didn't you try to get it back or sell it by talking to him? It is still in your and his name, right?"

I look down at my hands, "See, we were not married then; it didn't make sense to buy the house in both of our names. So he said we should buy the house in his name, and later once married, we can work on the house deeds." Admitting it out loud only fills me with shame and realization of how naive and stupid I was.

He looks at me, surprised. "Prachi, you are one of the smartest people I have ever met. How can you do something this stupid? He duped you for all your money. He used you as a goose who gives golden eggs."

Okay, this conversation is becoming intolerable now. But since he is my husband now, I guess he deserves to know, "I was young and blind in love."

His expression makes me feel small. He looks disappointed in me. "Prachi, I understand you were in love. But you made all that money and saved even when you were a teenager. Do you know what teenagers actually do? They do drugs and parties. And you let it go like that?"

This time I give him a stern look while struggling to say anything. After a few seconds, I finally say, "Okay, let me explain it to you the way you will understand. You say you love me, and I mean the world to you, right?"

He nods, and then I continue, "So if I say now that we should buy a penthouse in Bangalore together and I ask you to pay for it but buy it in my name, will you deny it?"

Realization fills in his eyes. I didn't want to use his feelings and throw it in his face, but I guess this is the only way he would understand. He finally says, "I will never deny you anything or even question your motives. I understand. I guess if you ever leave me in the coming days, I won't be able to do anything to hurt you or harm you."

I look away from him, and he puts his finger on my chin and tilts it towards him. He looks like he is struggling to ask something, "Do you still love him?"

Oh! My face softens automatically because this must be painful for him. I now know how much he loves me and that he will go to any extent for me. And it makes my heart beat faster than ever. I never thought anyone would love me like this. True, his showing methods are outrageous, but still, he loves me. I finally reply to put him at ease, "No, Arjun. I don't love him anymore. But I guess I didn't want to do anything about it because I didn't want to waste my energy on such a painful thing. I could have fought, but after I came out of that apartment, I wanted the pain to go away. Money is not a big deal. I have earned much, much more than that. It's that two of the most important people in my life betrayed me together. Madhav and Shristi were the only people I had in my life after my parents. It damaged me from inside, and I didn't want to look back ever again."

He releases a sigh of relief pulls me to his chest again, and kisses my forehead. I love sleeping in his arms. It makes me feel safe, which is why I always sleep all over him every night.

24

Arjun- Raging heart

I haven't blinked my eyes the whole night. I kept staring at my beautiful wife. She is smiling in her sleep while sleeping in my arms. But I cannot get my mind off the conversation we had.

Tonight she also accepted the fact that I love her unconditionally. I didn't like how she put it out, but I guess she was trying to explain her actions to her Ex.

But just because she didn't do anything about it doesn't mean I won't. It must have hurt like a bitch when you see two of the only people you call important outside family fucking with your trust. Till tonight I wanted to love her and make her fall in love with me. But now that it is impossible. I will have to love her and make her trust me enough to rely on me. I can live with that.

I will make those two fuckers beg for her forgiveness. They ruined anything about love and trust for her in life. Plus, they made a fool of such a smart and beautiful person. The whole night I kept looking at her sleeping form. She looks so soft and breakable. But I also got to know today that she is invincible. Nothing will break her; at least, it won't be visible to the world.

While deep in my thoughts, she twitches in my grip and starts crawling above me. I smile because she does this every night. She rubs herself on me in sleep, and I start getting hard instantly. I am in a hard-on state every moment she is around me. As she says, I have become a sex maniac. Only if she ever understands that it's all because of her.

When the sun starts to rise, I push her to bed and remove her clothes while she moans in her sleep. I start worshipping her body, and like every time, she wakes up with a jolt when I am between her legs. But for the first time today, she didn't seem surprised. She gave me a sexy smile, "I am starting to like my wake-up alarm husband."

I stare at her with an open mouth. I smile, and something moves in my chest. It's my fucking heart. I fucking love this woman. This morning, I saw the reflection of my love in her eyes. She feels loved, cared and protected.

We finish our morning routines and go down to breakfast with her parents. Surprisingly my whole family is also here, and we have a big breakfast feast. I finally told Prachi that I needed to go to Bangalore to handle work there. And she agreed to go with me, but I think she missed Ria.

They both are inseparable. And they both love their work which amazes me.

When we reached Bangalore, I realized this was the first time she would visit my apartment. I wish I could make love to her on every surface of my apartment or our apartment. But we both have to go to work. We enter inside, and she looks all around with awe. The look on her

face tells me she likes what she sees. And I add to the point, "We can redecorate it however you want. We can also make a wall of your assets here, you know."

She looks at me and smiles sadly, "You really love me a lot, don't you?"

I match her smile, take her in my arms, and kiss her lips. "You have no idea how much. But I want you to know that I don't expect anything in return other than your presence in my life. Forever!"

She buries her face in my chest. I give her a tour of the whole apartment. And I keep the bedroom for last, "Please make it our home. I want your essence in every corner of this place."

She nods with an overwhelmed expression.

"Come, baby. Let's get changed and get back to work. Because I want you in this bed as soon as possible, okay? Please don't keep me waiting." I give her a pleading look, to which she smirks and replies, "What if you are the one stuck at work?"

"Fuck work. I have waited so long for you to be in my arms, I don't care about anything. If it was up to me, you wouldn't be leaving this bed for weeks. But I know how much you love your work, so I am being lenient." I give her the pout face that she usually makes and it has her laughing.

Again music to my ears.

We get back to work, and now I know I have some important matters to give attention to. I called one of my contacts and asked for all the details related to Madhav.

25

Prachi- Gratitude

After so many years, today morning, I felt an emotion that I almost forgot existed. I have been feeling anxious since then. When I entered Arjun's apartment today, I was in awe. It was nothing as I expected. I thought his apartment would be manly and luxurious. But it was simple and organized. And then he asked me to make it our home. Redecorate it. He even suggested making a wall of books for me. He had been showing his love for me, but I was not taking it seriously. But he has been persistent and never shies away from showing his feelings for me.

And even though I haven't reciprocated the same to him, he has not complained once.

Initially, I thought he would stop putting effort after a while. But last night, when I confessed everything to him, he understood me and was even angry for my pain. In comparison, his own past is full of ghosts. I am more confused now. I know I am starting to fall for him. But I am scared. All the what-if questions have started arising in my brain.

Ria comes into my office and hugs me excitedly, "Hey, beautiful! How are you?"

I hug her back and reply, "I missed you. I am not used to staying away from you. And it is difficult to focus on work when you are not around."

She looks at me with an open mouth, "What have you done to my best friend? Where is she?"

"What?"

"Oh, come on, Prachi! You have never expressed your emotions to me like this. You usually growl at me for making your life hectic and chaotic." She gives me a cheeky smile.

Then I realize I have not only closed my emotions for love, but I have also closed them for everyone around me, even my parents. I feel a pang of guilt inside my heart. I was not like this. I was always an introvert, but I used to be lively.

Ria places a hand over my shoulder, and I look at her, "It is okay, Prachi. You are coming back to your real self. And believe me, it makes me very happy for you. You are glowing, babe. Don't overthink anything. You are falling in love. And it is visible on your face. I knew Arjun was the one who would bring you back from the cage you created for yourself."

Damn it! I am crying so much nowadays. Since the day of marriage, all I am doing is crying. All the tears I reserved from past years are fighting to get out. I hug Ria back, "Ria, I am sorry I never showed you how important you are to me. I am so grateful to have you in my life. You

came into my life when I needed a strong wall to hold on to. And you became that without any complaints, yet I never thanked you for it."

She laughs in a sarcastic way which surprises me, "Prachi, you have no idea what you mean to me or what your family means to me. I was all alone in this world before you came into my life.

Now I have a place to call home and people to call my own. Your parents have adopted me, and they love me so much that I want to stay permanently with them. And all these became possible only because of you. So you don't have to thank me for anything. You are my best friend, and I would die for you."

"Now tell me, what is bothering you? You looked like you were about to break down." God, she always sees through me. I nod at her.

"Before I tell you what is bothering me, I want to tell you about my past." I told her everything I talked about with Arjun last night and everything about Madhav and Shristi. And again, I see the same anger and pain on Ria's face that I saw on Arjun's face last night.

After staying quiet for a long time, she reaches out and takes my hand, saying, "You are afraid of falling in love with Arjun." And I nod.

"Prachi, I know you have control issues. But you need to accept that you will never be able to control your future. You can only live in the present. So embrace these feelings and free fall. I know for a fact that these Dixit siblings are a force you cannot fight. Better go with the flow."

I look at her, surprised. I have wanted to ask her about her and Rahul, but I never wanted to pry.

But since she has given me a hint, I ask directly, "So what's going on with you? I have noticed that you have a good bond with Rahul."

"Hmm... Well, I never shared this with you because you never asked. As you met Arjun in Goa, I also met Rahul there. But it was an introduction kind of meeting there. But on the housewarming day, we met again and became friends. He was fun to hang out with and always behaved like a gentleman. I felt attracted to him, but I didn't want to lose his friendship. That first time we went to the club Rahul, Sameera, and I went to another club after you left. We got so wasted that we crossed some boundaries that night. We both woke up in my apartment

together in bed."

She paused a moment, "Since then, it has become complicated."

I hug her, "It will all work out with time."

"I know. Let's get back to work. By the way, tomorrow we have that meeting with Mr. Patrick. You have been working on the proposal for the whole last month. This will be the biggest project for us till now. So I want you completely relaxed today. Do as much meditation as you can. Okay?"

she gives me an assuring smile, and I smile at her back.

We both get back to work. Tomorrow is an important day for our company. If we bag this deal, our company will reach the top list in the global market. I have worked hard on this proposal. I need to bring my A-game tomorrow. Ria and I discussed the proposal the whole afternoon. I am

already anxious about tomorrow. After everything seems good, I leave the office and leave for my apartment. I pack a bag of necessities and go to Arjun's apartment. The moment I enter the apartment, my cell starts to ring, and I smile while I receive it, "Hey! I just got back home. How is

your day going?"

"My day is going at a very slow pace. How come you are back so early? I thought I would have to kidnap you from your office in the evening."

"Ha ha... I have an important meeting tomorrow. So Ria sent me home to relax. I need to be well prepared. So I came home.", I replied. Did I refer to his apartment as 'home'?

"Great! I will be on my way then. I will see you soon."

"Don't you have work to do?" Even though I was excited at the thought of him coming home sooner, I asked.

"I can manage to work from home if required, but I want to be with you. Now freshen up, and I'll be there soon. Okay?"

I go to the bathroom and take a shower. I found a beautiful lingerie set in my wardrobe in Jabalpur before leaving today morning, which I packed in my bag. It's in soft red, and the lace fabric has a beautiful pattern. I wear it and cover myself in a robe. I blow dry my hair and go to the kitchen. I want some coffee to diffuse the stress, but I find some chamomile tea in his pantry.

So I brew a cup for myself and sit on the balcony attached to his bedroom. When I see my apartment balcony, a smile forms on my face. He has been watching me from here for so many years. I habitually read a book on my balcony while drinking a coffee or bourbon.

A pair of tan veiny hands wrap around my shoulders from the back, and I smell the familiar cologne. It's minty and lime, and I feel a warmth in my chest. He whispers near my ears, "I see you found my favorite place, yeah?"

He bites my earlobes, and I start giggling, "Yeah, I can see why. The view is awesome from here. Though now it's empty. How often you used to watch me from here?"

"Mostly on weekends when you used to read books or work on your laptop. Other days the timings didn't match much.", He chuckles. "In your eyes, I must be looking like a serial stalker."

26

Prachi- So fucking hot!

"Arjun, you are a serial stalker!" I tell him, widening my eyes, and his face falls. I sit in his lap and kiss him, "But I am glad you are my stalker. Despite everything that has happened between us and everything you have done to me, I can't ignore the fact that I feel happy and safe with

you. So if you being my stalker is what gave me this life, then I am grateful to have it."

His face becomes hard, and I don't know what he is thinking, so I kiss his jaw to ease him up.

He takes my hand, places it over his heart, kisses my forehead, and says, "I love you, baby, and I am yours. And you are mine."

I smile and say, "I am yours too."

Life is weird. When you weave dreams and put effort into building them, you get thrown down and thrashed. But when you lose hope, life gives you what you always wanted in a different way and a different shape. I guess all pain I went through with Madhav and Shristi; life knew I didn't

deserve what I wished for. So it gave me Ria, and Arjun and his loving family. My parents are the best, and now everything else is best too.

Arjun caresses my arm, asking, "So you have an important meeting tomorrow?"

"Yeah. We are presenting our proposal to Evans Group Industries from the U.S. tomorrow. If we bag this deal, it will be the biggest contract for our company, and we will rank up in the global market. We are going to showcase our digital marketing strategy for their product and how it will increase their brand awareness as well as increase their sales."

"That's great. You will do great. You want me to have a look at it?" he asks. Wow! I never expected that he would show interest in my work. Plus, I could practice my presentation with him.

"Will you be okay with that? You must be having your work."

"Nah! I am good. I have a few emails to reply to, but I can do that later. Show me your presentation."

"Okay. I could use the practice. Shall I present it to you? You can give me your honest opinion and feedback.", I tell him, and he smiles and nods.

We go to his home office, and he sets up the projector with my presentation. I started explaining the proposal and our marketing strategy. And he listened to me with sincere attention. And practicing it with him makes me more confident for tomorrow. Once I finish, I wait for him to say something, but he stays quiet. So I ask, "What do you think?"

He stands up and walks around the table, "Well, your proposal is very good. I am impressed with your marketing strategy too. But why have you quoted your price so low?"

"Well, if I reduce the prices, they would definitely consider us. Plus, our prices will need to be much lower than the companies in the U.S. Otherwise, why would he consider making a deal with an Indian company." I explained my reasons to him.

He remains quiet for a few seconds and then tells me, "Prachi, your strategies are 100% going to work. And as much as I know about the Evans group, they are a big company. They would prefer to pay well and get better quality than going for a lesser cost. Lowering the cost may

create a doubt about the quality of work you will be delivering."

Hmm... I think through what he said, and it makes sense. Mr. Patrick is a very peculiar person, as I have heard. People consider him the perfect example of a true businessman. So I asked Arjun again, "What you say makes sense. So, according to you, what should be the quoting price?"

"The way I understand, you should increase your quote price by 20%. so you can make a good amount of profit and it will still be less than what other companies will be quoting. In this industry, it is very important to value your worth. Sometimes you have to stand your ground and value the quality you deliver rather than trying to convince the client. It builds the client's confidence in you."

Hmm... I knew he was intelligent and amazing at what he did, but he never showed it off. And he treats everyone very well, even his staff. That shows the true gentleman in him. I smile at him and hug him, "Thank you for helping me. I feel pretty confident now. I will implement your suggestions."

"Well, I must say, you look so damn sexy in your work mode. It was very difficult for me to concentrate on your presentation." He pulls me close, and I feel his hardness over my abdomen. He pulled the loose end of the rope keeping my robe intact, and I knew what he would find. The moment he sees the lingerie, he gasps.

27

Arjun- Thetemptress

She looks like a temptress. On her pale and soft skin, she wears red lingerie that looks so beautiful. So creamy and yummy. She has always been wearing plain bras and panties since we got married. Except for the time on our honeymoon. It intrigues me. She has been showing emotions and expressing her thoughts today. I growl at the thought, "Baby, are you wearing this for me?"

She looks at me with an angry expression, "Oh no! I am wearing it for a photoshoot I have scheduled this evening."

"If you think anyone will ever see you in this, then you will be visiting me in prison, sweetheart." I push her robe from her shoulders. I take her elbow and twist it not to hurt her but to get her closer to me; her boobs are thrusting on my chest, "Now answer me, baby."

She looks into my eyes and gives me a smirk, "Yes, I am wearing it for you."

Hearing her say it makes my heart race. Finally, the woman I love shows her emotions for me, making me go wild. I kiss her lips and dive my tongue into her mouth. I bite her lower lip just enough to create a zap of pain but not to break her skin. She moans loudly into my mouth. I pick her up and settle her on my desk. I swipe all the files away from the table and make her lie on the surface. She breathes heavily. I am going crazy by seeing her in this vulnerable position.

She sits up and reaches for me to remove my shirt, but my patience is at the limit. So I remove all my clothes myself and latch on to her. I start licking her earlobes and move towards her neck. I rip her bra and start sucking on her boobs and biting them. Her moans keep making me wilder. I lick her tight abdomen and tear her red panties. I latch on to her core, and she starts screaming as I bite her slightly. I push two fingers inside her, hitting the spot that makes her crazy. She starts thrashing her arms to the side of the table.

"Arjun, please... now..."

I chuckle at her desperation. I take hold of her arms and push them above her head. I kiss her lips and push myself inside her in one thrust. She stills, and her eyes start brimming with tears of ecstasy. I start moving inside her with all the energy contained inside my body, and she comes in a few seconds. I watch her face as she comes down from the height of her orgasm. But without giving her time to get together of her senses, I start thrusting again. I rub her clit when I feel close to reaching my orgasm.

"Come for me, baby."

"Arjun... I can't. It is too.... intense." When she comes, I come with her. I watch her spread on the table and know I won't be able to focus on my work here anymore. She looks at her ripped lingerie and gives me a pout, "I liked that one."

"I will buy you a fucking lingerie shop if you want. But don't expect me to unwrap my present slowly, keeping the wrapping paper intact."

She laughs, "You are a moron!" I reply in my usual signature style, "Only for you, baby."

I pick her up in my arms and take her to the bathroom ensuite of our bedroom.

After we cleaned ourselves, Prachi moved around the kitchen, and I watched over her. She goes over from cupboard to cupboard. She opens the refrigerator and the pantry shelves. "Babe, what are you looking for?" I ask

"I am looking at all the ingredients you have so that I can cook something for our dinner," she says absent-mindedly. "Babe, you don't have to cook. We can order in."

"Oh no! I don't want to eat take-out. Eating out once in a while is okay, but I don't do well with it every day. What would you like to eat? We have mushrooms and veggies. I can make mushroom fried rice with the things you have in your pantry."

I observe her for a while and reply, "I am okay with anything. Tell me if you need any help."

"It's alright. You can reply to your emails in the meantime. Are you allergic to anything?" she asks, looking in my direction. I shake my head. I bring my laptop and sit on the kitchen slab.

It feels weird watching someone cook food in my apartment. I never ate here. I either always order take-out or eat out. There was never even anything in my pantry. I told my caretaker that my wife and I would come to stay, and I think she stocked the pantry. I have only made coffee, tea, or packaged soup in my kitchen. I watch her chopping the veggies throwing everything in the pan and tossing the ingredients. I didn't even know that she could cook.

Curious to know, I asked her, "How did you learn to cook with your nerdy schedule?"

She gives me a stern look, "I was never a person to ask for things. And I used to observe a lot when my mom used to cook. Whenever I was hungry, even as a child, I didn't like bothering anyone. I used to whip something myself with whatever was available. Plus, even in my college days, I disliked the food served in my college canteen. So in my dorm, too, I kept a hot pot and used to cook for myself and my roommate. It was cheaper than eating out and much healthier."

Hmm... I understand now. She likes everything in her control and always likes to do things herself. "Don't you get exhausted by doing everything by yourself? I am just imagining what you must be doing at work. You must be doing things by yourself there too."

She laughs at my analogy, "So you picked that, yeah! I have OCD, and keeping things in order and tasks done in a particular way is a compulsion for me. I was very bad at delegating my work in the office. That's why Ria puts work on my plate so I don't end up doing everything myself.

Even though I have a PA, it is Ria who mostly handles me at work because I don't know when to stop. And to answer your question, yes, it is exhausting, but I am used to it. And if I don't do things by myself, I start getting irritated. Being exhausted is better than being irritated."

I nod to her and focus on my emails. After a few minutes, Prachi plates the food and sets one in front of me. I smile at her because the food arranged on the plate looks beautiful and smells amazing. I set aside my laptop and picked up the spoon. Once she is sitting with me, I take a bite, and I freeze. I am a fan of Chinese food, but this was by far the best mushroom-fried rice I ever had. A moan escapes from me, which surprises me. I take hold of her hand and kiss the top of it.

"This is the best fried rice I have ever had. I am amazed. What else are you good at? Or is there anything you are bad at ever?"

She smiles, "I have many flaws but thank you. Now eat."

We eat our food silently. I put away all the utensils in the dishwasher while she cleans the kitchen slab. And for the rest of the evening, we both focus on our work while sitting close to each other.

28

Prachi- The celebration

Ria and I are hugging and bouncing up and down in our office. After I presented our proposal and strategies to Mr. Patrick, he agreed to accept it. And he was very impressed with our plans. Even though we proposed a two-year contract, he countered, saying he wanted to extend it to five years and negotiate the prices after the initial two years. Bagging a five-year contract with such a big global company was a first for us.

We immediately sent the details to our law department to draw up the contracts. And had an announcement made to all the employees. We ordered food and drinks for everyone to celebrate. After a while, Ria tells me we should call everyone and have a night out to celebrate, and I agree. She makes the call to Sameera and Rahul, and I call my husband.

He picks up after the third ring, and it is difficult to contain my excitement, "Hey! What's my handsome husband doing right now?". I realize I am flirting with him, which brings me a different excitement.

He chuckles and sighs for a reason, "I finished a meeting and was going for a coffee with Rahul. I miss you a lot.

What are you doing? How was your meeting?"

"I am missing you too. We got the deal. And not only that, Mr. Patrick asked to re-draw the contracts for five years. We celebrated in our office with everyone. And I want to thank you for helping me yesterday. You were right; our previous quote price was too low."

"That's amazing news, baby. Congratulations! But will the five-year contract continue with the same quote price?"

"Oh no, no. We are drawing up the contract with the condition of renegotiating the prices after the year mark period."

"That's great! I am so happy for you guys. We should celebrate.", he replies.

"Yeah! Ria talked with Sameera and Rahul. We are planning to meet in the evening. I am not sure which place they have chosen yet but will you make it? Please, pretty please." I try to be cute.

He laughs and says, "Well, now I have to make it 'cause you said pretty please. Shall I pick you up from the office?"

I think about it, "Well, I guess going to and fro will be a waste of time. I will go along with Ria, and you can come together with Rahul."

He replies okay, and we hang up. I focus on my work again to finish before we leave tonight.

Ria made reservations for us and reached there, but both of us were in formals. We didn't have time to change. I was wearing a navy blue pencil skirt, a purple shirt, and a navy blue blazer. I dressed for my presentation while Ria wore black trousers pants along with a

red blouse and a black blazer. We both felt dressed funny. And as it was a Thursday night, the bar was moderately crowded. Sameera was already waiting for us. I hug her, and she congratulates us. At the same time, Arjun and Rahul enter the bar. And at the same moment, I look at him dressed in formal, looking hot as hell. When I saw him in the morning, I felt butterflies in my stomach. He comes close and kisses me on my forehead, placing his hand on my back. I close the distance automatically. Both he and Rahul congratulate us. Rahul gives me a kiss on my cheek, "How is my favorite sister-in-law?"

"I am your only sister-in-law Rahul. I am good. How are you doing?" I ask by hugging him, and Arjun doesn't move his hand from my back the whole time.

Rahul replies, "I am good as well. So what should we drink tonight?"

We order tequila shots. When our shots arrive, we all toast to good times and drink. After the fourth shot, they all start talking in drunk voices. I rest my head on Arjun's head and watch them with a smile on my face. I have never been talkative, but being with all these people makes me happy. And this current moment is only possible because of Arjun. I sigh and listen to them all chatting happily.

I watch Ria, Rahul, and Sameera fighting over who is better in the business world, "Men or Women", and I laugh at their arguments. Arjun being mischievous keeps spraying gasoline on the fire in their argument. I watch him enjoying this moment while he caresses my shoulder with his fingers. At the same moment, his cell phone starts to ring. He takes it out, and I can see it's an unknown number. A weird look crosses his face, and he mutters that he has to take the call. He gets up from his seat and walks out of the bar. Why would he tense up because of a call from an unknown number? Maybe it was because of work. He returns in a few minutes, and I ask, "Is everything ok?"

He looks at me and gives me a reassuring smile saying, "Yeah, all good. It was a client." He is trying to look calm and collected, but his body is still tense. Maybe something at work is bothering him. I press a kiss to his cheeks, and he eases up. I feel good about myself for the effect I have on him. This is the first time I have ever felt like this. Like my presence can make someone so happy. That even a mere touch of mine can make the blood flow faster in their body.

He holds me close to him, and I melt when he kisses me on top of my head. How can this one person bring so much change to my life? I linger over the question and feel Ria's gaze on me.

She looked at me with a smile, and I knew what she was telling me. She is telling me to let go and fall. And I try to search for the uneasy feeling in my heart. It's gone. I am not scared anymore. I sigh again and enjoy the moment.

29

Prachi- Blast from the past

It's been two months since I got married, and it is blissful. Ria and I have bagged a few more contracts in the office with global companies. We have hired more employees too because of the workload. Arjun makes me feel like I am living a dream. He has deactivated my alarm now permanently. He wakes me up every morning worshipping my body and workouts with me too.

He makes sure I eat my breakfast. Now we go together to the café in front of our apartment to get coffee before leaving for the office. And every night, we talk about work once we are back at our home. Sometimes, he makes me sit over his lap on the balcony bench while I read a book. He even makes me read it aloud for him to listen. And every night, I sleep over his chest after he makes sweet, sweet love to me. He is becoming more dominant daily in bed, and I am enjoying it to the fullest.

It's a Friday afternoon, and Arjun said we would be going for a weekend getaway. And as usual, he likes to keep me in surprise. I wrapped up all my meetings sooner so that I could go home. Take a shower before we left wherever the hell he was taking me. I kiss Ria on her cheek and tell her about my plans. I get into the elevator to get out of the building. I try booking a cab, but it is difficult in Bangalore. Once I get out of the building, I try again, and I feel someone approaching me. I look to my side and see Shristi standing there.

I am shocked, and my mouth remains open. She comes and stands very close to me, "Hi Prachi. It's been a long time, yeah! You look good."

Even though she is talking calmly, her eyes seem cold. I get my nerves in control; looking at her brings back too many painful emotions. I didn't even know how to respond to her cause I was too shocked to see her. I try to reply to her calmly, "What are you doing here, Shristi?"

"I came here to talk to you."

What could she have to talk about after all that has happened? "I don't have anything to talk to you about. I am in a hurry right now. So excuse me, I need to go." I tell her and go back to my cellphone, trying to book a cab. God! Why can't I get a cab sooner?

She looks at me for a while and then says in a stiff voice, "Come on, Prachi. I want to talk to you. We can go to a café and have a coffee and talk. I have my car here. I will drop you off afterward, too. It's half an hour. I think we need to clear the things between us. After all, we were best friends."

Oh, the guts of this woman. When she sees the anger in my face, she makes a sad face and says again, "I want to talk. Please."

I think for a while. Because I was excited to spend the weekend with Arjun, I left the office early. So I thought half an hour wouldn't make any changes. And I was now curious about what she had to talk about, that too after so many years. It's been nearly three and half years now since I last saw her when she and Madhav kicked me out of that apartment.

I nod at her, and she takes me to her car. She gets into the driver's side, and I get into the passenger seat. I try to put on my seat belt when I feel a hit blow on my head from the back.

And I turn towards her losing my senses slowly. I try feeling my head on the back with my hand, and I feel my fingers wet. Blood starts flowing down the back side of my neck. Suddenly, everything starts to blur. I try hard not to lose my senses. I feel the car moving while I take my blooded hand and try to hold Shristi's hands over the steering wheel. She jerks my hand, saying, "Sit quietly bitch if you want to stay alive."

The tone in her voice shocks me, and slowly everything turns black.

30

Prachi- Fucking frying pan!

I feel my head hurting like hell. I try to open my eyes, it feel disoriented. Water splashed on my face harshly. I cannot even remember what happened to me and how I ended up in this situation.

"Wake up bitch!"

I move my eyes towards the voice. I try hard to concentrate, and slowly it all returns to me. Me standing outside my office building trying to get a cab, and Shristi was convincing me to talk. Oh my God! I am such a fool. I look at Shristi's face, and I see anger and evil.

I cannot form anything to say at all, and in a husky voice, I ask the obvious question, "What do you want from me? Why are you doing this?"

"Oh, Miss Genius wants to know why I am doing this. You have been living the life you have always dreamed of, haven't you? You have a successful career. You are running a company as you always wanted. You have all the money you don't even know how to use as you still dress like a nerd. You married a rich man and are living a happy life.

And do you have any idea how I have been living all these years? DO YOU?"

I try to make sense of her words. Anger floods in my veins, "Why will it matter to me? After everything you and Madhav did to me after you guys betrayed me, I was the one on the roads. I was the one picking my life from rock bottom. And now you have stooped this low. Kidnapping me and injuring me on the pretense of having coffee. Have you lost your mind, Shristi? I still don't understand what you want from me. I left and went out of your and his life."

She slaps me hard on my face. And I try to move to hit back. Then I realize I am sitting on a chair with my hands and legs bound to it. What the fucking hell? "Shristi, have you lost your mind? You know you can go to jail for this?"

She laughs maniacally. I look at her. I go back to that day when I felt broken. I calm myself. I look at my surroundings and realize I am in the same apartment that Madhav and I bought together. They change everything in the house. They still use the same appliances and furniture, but the decor changes. She has kept me in the bedroom. If she was kidnapping me, then why bring me here? This is the easiest way to get caught because this is the first place they will come looking for me. But how will anyone know it is her that has kidnapped me? I and Arjun were supposed to go together. He must be so worried right now. I don't know if he will be able to find me. I focus back on Shristi as my brain starts working. I know how to fight. I need to find a way to escape her. She doesn't look normal. The way she is talking and behaving, it seems she is mentally unstable. My mind goes back to the last time I was with her. The way she slapped me last time, too, and the way she was fighting, she was never stable. No normal person behaves like this. If I can trick her somehow and escape, I can get out of this mess. I don't know where she kept my bag. How did she get me inside the apartment? She couldn't have carried me here alone. Is Madhav doing this to me her? If that is the case, then my escape will be very difficult. Maybe I can keep her talking without enraging her anymore. I have to stay conscious from now on. She is holding a frying pan in her hand. And it coats the end of it with blood. She hit me with a frying pan in the car. She has kept a cleaver knife on the side table near the bed. Okay, this looks bad.

I make my voice as soft as possible and ask, "What happened to you, Shristi? You were never like this. We stayed together for four years in college. We were best friends. Why did you do all that to me years ago, and why are you doing this to me now?" Even though I am asking her in a steady tone, my inside is shivering right now. What if she kills me before anyone can find me?

My parents won't survive this. And Arjun, Oh God Arjun! I love him so much, and I can't imagine the stress he must be going through right now. I haven't even told him I have fallen in love with him. My eyes start to tear up at that thought.

Shristi brings me back to the present by throwing the pan against the wall. She looks like she is about to break down, "It is all because of you. From day one of college, it was me who loved Madhav. I liked him and wanted to date him. But you took his attention first. And then you both always used to spend time in our dorm. It was so painful to watch you both together every day.

After the first semester, you spent most of your time in the library, working and studying. Madhav used to wait for you in our dorm for hours. We got close, and I was so happy. I asked him to leave you so I could have him all to me. And guess what he said? He said that he needs you in his life because you are smart. That you will help him get everything that he needs in his life. I was heartbroken again. He knew you were already earning a lot of money while studying in college. We continued being together behind your back and eventually, he confessed to me that he loved me in his final year. He said he was going to break it up with you. But he expressed his worry about securing a job and his desire to buy a house soon to marry me. After that, it was I who planned everything. I convinced him that we could use you to get the money and buy the house. And everything was going good till you found us that day."

She laughed sarcastically and paused for some time, "I felt such a relief that day. I finally had Madhav all to myself. Every moment you spent with Madhav was like a slow poison to me. After that, Madhav and I were happy. We both had decent jobs and were able to pay for the remaining payment of the house. We got married. But after the first year itself, Madhav started acting weird. He was always working and focusing on money. Last year the company I was working for went bankrupt, and I lost my job. And Madhav became more stressed than before and started distancing from me. I suggested that we should have a kid. I love him, and I always dreamed of having a family with him, but he denied that, saying we can't afford to have a kid right now. And last month, Madhav lost his job."

She looked at me with rage as if she was going to kill me right now, "It was all because of you."

Yup! She has gone mental. "How is it because of me?"

She comes and yanks my hair; I scream in pain, "It was your husband who took over the company and fired him."

What? Arjun wouldn't do this? Right! He was angry that day when I told him everything. He said that Madhav and

Shristi would pay for what they did to me. I try to think about it all. Would Arjun buy a whole damn company to get Madhav fired? I know what Arjun is capable of. He is like an apex predator, like a lion of the jungle. He doesn't stop until he gets his prey in his claws. And once he gets hold of his prey, he tears through its neck, giving a clean death.

Shristi punches me in the face to get my attention again. My head is throbbing, and my jaw hurts a lot. I am sure I am bleeding right now. I am going to lose my senses again due to extreme pain.

Shristi says, "Because of you and your so-called rich husband, I have lost everything in life. We are going to lose this house too. And now you are going to solve everything."

"How can I solve anything? Shristi, I know nothing about this. And I don't think Arjun can fire Madhav without any reason. I can talk to Arjun, and we can sort this all out."

"No, there is no sorting required. We were not able to meet the end of our finances. We were not able to pay the monthly payments to the bank after I lost my job. Madhav did some small scams to get the money. And your dear husband found that and fired him. Not only did he fire Madhav from his job, but he also got him blacklisted from the industry and sued him for the scam. He is going to go to jail."

I try to take deep breaths. This bitch is going to kill me soon. I need to find an escape. But she continues while I look for something or a way to fight her, "How is this my fault? If Madhav managed to do such a thing, someone would have detected him at some point. Why are you blaming me for this? And I can't help you with the situation you both have put yourself in."

"Oh, you will fulfill your purpose as always. You will give me all the money you have by which I can pay for this house and secure my future with Madhav. And you will ask your husband to take back the case against Madhav." I feel disgusted listening to her.

All the anger from past years starts driving my mouth without thinking about the consequences, "Was that all I was to both of you? A free bank account with an unlimited source of money. You were my only friend. I trusted you. If you had told me in the first place that you liked Madhav, I

wouldn't have dated him. Don't you think after everything you have done to me in the past, what you are doing right now is going to blow up in your face? You both used me for years. After that day, I had nothing left in my life. You guys stole all the money I kept in the joint account too.

And now you want me to give you all the money I have earned with hard work. And by the way, if Madhav digs his grave by doing those scams, then I don't think even Arjun will be able to stop it."

At the same time, the doorbell rings, and she picks up the pan and hits my head from the front; this time, everything becomes black. I hear the door opening and people coming through, but I am not able to keep my eyes open anymore. Suddenly, I hear Arjun's voice, and I move into darkness, embracing it.

31

Arjun- Baffled

I have been calling Prachi for the past hour, but she has switched off her cell phone. I called Ria to ask about her whereabouts, and she told me that Prachi left at 3 PM to come home. When I don't find her in our apartment, I get impatient by now. I called her parents, thinking she had gone to Jabalpur for some emergency that I didn't know about. But they talked normally. I didn't want to make them worry, so I dropped the call.

I reach her office and go directly to Ria's cabin. Looking at me, she stands abruptly, "Arjun, what are you doing here? Weren't you and Prachi leaving for Goa as planned by now?"

"She is missing Ria. Her cell phone is off. She is not in our house. I have been waiting for the past two hours. At first, I thought she was stuck in traffic, and her cellphone battery had died. But Prachi is very cautious about such things. She always charges her phone.

I called you, and you said she left at 3 PM. It is 6 PM now. It's been three hours."

Ria panics, "Do you think something has happened to her? Shall we report this to the police?"

In my mind, several possibilities are running; what if she went through an accident? Or was she in some trouble? How to find her in this big city? "I don't know. Maybe we should check with hospitals for any accidents. Do you know how she left? She usually comes to the office with you. She must have booked a cab. Will your building security help to know which cab she took?"

Ria thinks for a moment and says, "Yes. They have cameras outside the building entrance. And security guards are also always there. We can check the CCTV footage to know the cab number if required. Let's go ask them first."

I follow her robotically. My heart is racing at a speed that will give me an anxiety attack. Once we reached the security cabin, we questioned the person in charge. He checks the record for the security guard posted when Prachi left the building. He asks the guard to come, and Ria asks him by showing Prachi's picture. He looks at it for some time and recognizes her by name.

Ria continues, "So you know Prachi?"

The guard replies, "Yes, Madam. I saw her leaving today too. She searched for a cab and asked me if I could help her find one as she could not book one online. I tried, but no Rickshaws or cabs were available at that moment. Then a woman came, and Prachi Madam was talking to her.

After a few minutes, they both left together in a car."

She left with some woman. But she would have called me or texted me if she had some plans. I still feel like something very wrong is happening and that Prachi is in trouble. I conveyed the same to Ria, and she said we should watch the camera footage. We asked the security in charge to show us the footage around 3 PM. I watch the screen and squint. A woman who looks about the same age as Prachi is talking to her. But both their body language seems tense.

It looks like Prachi is trying to avoid interacting with this woman. After a few minutes, I watch Prachi follow

the woman to a car. It seems like a swift red desire. They both get inside the car and after that, it looks like the woman has hit Prachi from behind as her head falls to the car's dashboard. My blood starts to boil, and Ria gasps at the same time.

Whoever this woman is, I am going to kill her. I asked the security in charge to zoom in on the camera and note the car number. And then, I took my cell phone and searched for one man who could help me at this point. Being in the construction and real estate business gives me the advantage of having contact with influential people. And that includes the police commissioner as well.

I make the call and explain everything. He immediately sends the best officer Rajiv to us. I also ask them to check the car number and who is the owner of it. I get a message with the car owner's details in a few seconds. The car owner is Madhav Misra. Shit! No no! This can't be happening. Prachi is in this mess because of me. But a woman took her. She must be Shristi.

Her former best friend and Madhav's wife.

Last month I hired a private detective to find all the details of Madhav. And his apartment details were also there. I told Officer Rajiv everything and told him we should start by going to his apartment. After watching the video footage, Rajiv tells me, "If she kidnapped your wife, then the last place she would take her is her apartment."

But my gut instinct is telling me she might be there. She might have come for revenge. And that apartment might be the best place for it as I made sure for them to lose it soon. So I insisted to Rajiv that we should check in the apartment first. I gave him the address details. I told Ria to stay in the office and inform Rahul and Sameera of everything. "Arjun, I want to come with you too. I am worried sick right now."

"No, Ria. Please trust me right now. Stay here or go to Rahul and Sameera and tell them everything and wait for me to call, okay? Don't worry. She will be alright. She has to be alright."

Ria nods as tears stream from her face. She holds my hand, "Arjun, she is everything to me. Please bring her back."

I place my other hand over hers, "I will. Try to calm down."

I follow Rajiv and get in his car. We get to the apartment location. And Rajiv is a police officer, so we quickly get inside the building. Once we reach the door, Rajiv rings the calling bell, and my heart is drumming inside. I feel like I will collapse. My brain was not working. The door opens, and a woman peaks through the slightly open door. Rajiv shows his badge and tells her, "Madam, please open the door; we want to ask some questions."

She tries to shut the door entirely, but Rajiv stops her by pushing the door open. And we rush inside. I search through the rooms, and the moment I see Prachi, My heart stops. No! No!

I hear Shristi screaming at Rajiv to leave her. But my entire focus is on Prachi. She is lying on the floor sideways, bound to a chair. Her face looks distorted, and blood is streaming from the right side. I untie her from the chair and hold her in my arms. My palm feels wet when I hold her head in my hand. And I see blood.

Tears start to stream from my eyes. I take her in my arms and start to move outside when Rajiv tells me to put Prachi down. He has called for female officers and an ambulance. I am not going to wait till the ambulance reaches here.

At the same time, a few people come in with a stretcher. I place Prachi on it and follow them into the ambulance. I sit beside her and try rubbing her palm. She went through this because of me.

If I hadn't fired Madhav, she would be in my arms right now, happy. My chest hurts with pain and regret.

We reach the hospital, and they take her into the emergency unit. I stand outside, panicking the whole time. Ria calls me, and I tell her the hospital's name. I pace the corridor of the hospital.

God, please let her be okay. Please! Please! I keep chanting my prayers. In forty-five minutes, Ria, Rahul, and Sameera reach the hospital. The moment they see me, I exhale. Rahul comes to me and hugs me tight. I start howling like a baby, "It's all because of me. She might die because of me."

32

Arjun- Powerless

Ria and Sameera hold each other while Rahul keeps hold of me. Both Sameera and Rahul keep assuring me that Prachi will be fine. Ria keeps crying silently. I know how much Prachi means to her, so I get out of Rahul's arms and reach Ria. I hug her even though I don't have words to calm her down. I hold her while rubbing her back and cry myself.

After two hours, the doctor says, "Mrs. Dixit is in stable condition now. She had major injuries in two places on her head. One in the back and one in the front. We have treated her for now. Rest we can only tell once she is conscious again."

"How long will that take? How long will she be unconscious? Is everything else okay with her?" I started asking many questions to the doctor.

"Mr. Dixit, we can't exactly tell when as it is a head injury. But her vitals all seem fine. She has lost a lot of blood. So she is weak right now. We can only observe her condition from here onwards."

"Can I see her please?" I plead to him.

"Yes, Mr. Dixit. You can all go and see her, but I can only allow ten minutes. After that, only one person is to stay."

I exhale a breath I have been holding for a long time. Rahul grabs my shoulder and together we enter the room where Prachi is being observed. Just looking at her in this state gives me so much pain. It feels like someone has ripped out my heart from my chest.

She looks so vulnerable and weak. The love of my life, a fighter, is lying on a hospital bed, injured and unconscious. I feel like punching through a wall or killing someone at this moment.

I take hold of her hands and carefully place a kiss on her forehead. Bandages cover her forehead. And her jaw looks blue like someone crushed it with something. I can't express or compare any feeling in the world to the rage I am feeling right now. I asked all the others to

stay with Prachi and leave the room for a while. I dial Rajiv's number on my phone, "Hello, Mr. Dixit."

"Hello Officer Rajiv, please call me Arjun from here onwards. Is Shristi in custody right now? What about her husband, Madhav?" I ask with a tone that sounds dead cold.

"Arjun, both Shristi and Madhav are in our custody. But it seems Madhav didn't know anything about his wife kidnapping Prachi. He also confessed that his wife had been mentally unstable for quite a while. We are going to take all the actions as per law." replies Rajiv.

"I want them both locked up for a long time. And if Shristi is mentally unstable, make sure to lock her in an asylum for the rest of her life. After everything they did to my wife, there should be no mercy for both of them." I am no longer able to talk in a calm voice.

Once Rajiv confirms that he will see it, I disconnect the call and punch the nearest wall. Rahul comes to me at the same time. "Bhai, you need to calm yourself. I have called our parents and Prachi as well. They will reach in an hour or so. You need to get yourself together before they arrive. Let's go for a coffee."

I don't know how Prachi will react once she wakes up. Does she know that it was me who got Madhav fired, and because of that, Shristi kidnapped her? Will she leave me after knowing this?

I can't keep this from her, and if she decides to leave me, will I be able to let her go? I just got her in life.

Prachi's parents and I arrived at the hospital. Her mother is crying so hard, whereas her father is quiet. They sit near Prachi, and I leave the room and stand outside, unable to bear my mother's and mother-in-law's crying. My father-in-law comes out after a while and places a hand over my shoulder. I look at him and see the same pain in his eyes I am feeling now in my heart.

He asked me to sit with him. I take a seat, and he takes my hand and asks, "Will you tell me what happened? Who are the people who kidnapped her? How is my daughter in this condition?"

I choked at the thought of telling him everything. I feel my throat blocked, but I nod. I first told him everything Prachi said about Madhav and Shristi. And then I told him what I did and how I got Madhav fired from his job because of the embezzlement and scam he was doing. And after that how Shristi kidnapped Prachi in her deteriorated mental health.

I look into his eyes, "I promised her that I would make both of them pay for what they did to her and for using her money like that. I didn't know that she would get hurt like this." My father-in-law gives me a small smile and says, "Prachi never told us with this many details.

Honestly, if I had known, I would have done everything in my power to destroy them. So what you did was right.

You could have never thought that a woman would go to this extent. Are they both in jail right now?"

"They are in custody. Once Prachi wakes up and gives her statement, we can take further actions on them." I tell him.

At the same time, Ria comes toward us and informs us that Prachi is awake now. We all rush inside the room, and Prachi looks like she feels disoriented. She looks all around her, scanning her surroundings. I feel a crake in my heart.

33

Prachi-Regenerated

I open my eyes, and my head hurts, and I feel confused. Everything seems hazy for a while. I look around and see many people around me, even though everything is blurry. I look around the room, and slowly my vision gets clearer. I am lying on a bed with many machines beeping and needles stuck to my body. It seems like I am in a hospital. What happened to me? I find my parents and Ria sitting on my left; they look tired and worried. My mom looks like she has been crying for a long time with puffy red eyes. The same goes for Ria too. On the other hand, my father appears very tired; he scrunches his forehead as he looks at me. On my right side, my in-laws are sitting. My mother-in-law and Sameera also have red eyes. I look for Arjun and find him standing at the door. And looking at him, I suddenly start to remember everything.

Shristi took me with her and hit me with a frying pan. And then I remember sitting on a chair bound to it while she was behaving like a lunatic.

My mother is the one who talks first, "How are you feeling now, pumpkin?" Feeling her touch on my cheek makes me feel safe and better. I nod and say, "I am okay."

My voice sounds hoarse. I meet my eyes with Arjun again, and I see a raw pain in his eyes. He must have gone through hell in the last few hours. God knows what day and time it is. But I don't say or ask anything. A doctor comes into the room and asks me several questions. Starting with what's my name, what's my age, and if I remember how I got hurt. I reply to all. I know he is asking me all this because I got hit on my head. So this is an essential formality.

Everyone asks me to relax and feel better. Once the doctor leaves, my father is the one who asks, "Are you ready to tell us what happened? Arjun already told me everything about the past and present. I want to know how you got kidnapped and what happened during that time."

I look at Arjun, and he gives me an apologetic look. He told my father everything about me. At this point, I suppose it was supposed to come out.

I chuckle, sounding surprised by myself, "I didn't know I could be so stupid." I laugh again, "I never thought you could kidnap someone by using a bloody frying pan."

Everyone exchanged looks, and my father took my hand and nudged his chin for me to proceed, "I got out of my office building early as Arjun, and I were going to go somewhere that evening. I was trying to book a cab, but when I stood outside the building, I found Shristi standing there. She tried to convince me that she wanted to clear the air between us and wanted to have a coffee with me. I denied it at first, but she was persistent. So, I agreed, and we got inside her car. I was putting on my seat belt when I felt something hitting my head very hard, and in a few seconds, I lost my senses. When I woke up again, I was sitting on a chair bound to it with my hands and legs in her apartment. I don't know why she took me there after the kidnapping. Maybe she didn't plan it through, or she is a dumb lunatic. I was still in a lot of pain. She slapped me a few times while I was trying to keep her busy with talking. She seemed like she didn't know what she was doing. She was my best friend for a very long time so seeing her like that was weird and shocking for me. But I was trying to stall her. She had a frying pan and a cleaver knife on the side table. She kept ranting about all the things from college and how she was the one who fell in love with Madhav first. And that somehow I stole him from her nonsense. Then she told me about her current financial situation and how Madhav had lost his job. She wanted me to give her all the money I had right now. I got angry and asked why I would do that, and she punched me in the face. I think she hit me on my jaw."

I touch my jaw and feel a sharp pain there. But I continued telling them about the incident, "She kept telling me that it was all my fault. And after a while, the calling bell rang. I was alert at that moment, thinking Madhav had come too. But she again banged my head in the front with the frying pan, and I was out. And now I am here."

Everyone looks at me with wide eyes. I feel weird being the center of attention. My father nodded and said, "Well, it was stupid to go with her in her car, but I understand. You couldn't have thought she would go to this extent. But you handled things well, and all that matters is you are okay and safe now."

Everyone nods in agreement. After a while, I look at Arjun again and say, "I want to talk to Arjun in private." Arjun's face becomes cold, and everyone stands up and leaves the room. My mom goes the last after caressing my face and kissing me on my cheek.

34

Arjun- Walking into the fire

Once everyone leaves the room, I walk toward Prachi and sit near her bed. She looks at me with a penetrating gaze as if she is drilling a hole in my head. When I don't say anything, she folds her arms to her chest and says, "So what? Your wife wakes up in the hospital whom you claim to love so much, and you don't even kiss her?"

I look at her and instantly get up from my chair. I hold her face softly and kiss her lips. She winced, and I let her go. She takes my hand and asks me to sit near her on the bed.

"So tell me, why did you do it?" she asks me. I look her in the eyes, "Isn't it obvious?"

She gives me a stern look and comments in a clipped tone, "So I tell you about my past because I thought you deserved to know. And the next day, you run around trying to find my ex-boyfriend and buy the company he is working in. Then you get him investigated and fire him. Then to put the icing on the cake, you sue him for a scam. Is that it?"

I was thinking about how she was so calm from the moment she woke up. She has been controlling her emotions in front of others and me as well till now. She is slowly losing it. I was ready with my armor, "First of all, what they both did to you three years ago was completely wrong. And I didn't buy the company. I invested in it and became a partner in it. Yes, I had him investigated because I needed some reason to teach him a lesson. But when I found that he was conning a few of the company's clients, I hit the jackpot. Not only was I able to make him lose his job, but I also got to sue him for it. Plus, I checked his financials. He has a lot of debt. So yeah, I did it so they both wouldn't con someone else. I never thought you would get roped in it and hurt so badly."

I take her hand and kiss it, "I am sorry, Prachi. I know you are angry with me. I guess I am always hurting you. But that is never my intention, believe me. And you can be angry with me as much as you want. I will take all your wrath. But please don't hate me or leave me."

She laughs, and I look at her face. She is laughing even though she is wincing in between because of a busted lip and a bruised jaw.

"You know, when I woke up in that apartment and saw Shristi holding a frying pan in hand with my blood on it and a cleaver knife on the side table, I thought I was going to die. That she might chop my body off and dump it somewhere, I started thinking about what my parents and Ria would do. And at that moment, I only had one regret: I didn't get to tell you that I love you."

My heart is thumping in a slow rhythm now. I can count and feel each second pass. Did she say that she loves me? "What did you say?"

"I love you, Arjun. I love you just the way you are. And I guess I would do the same for you if I were in your situation. But I want to say that let's leave the past in the past. And honestly, Shristi would have come for me one day. She and Madhav were already in a terrible situation financially. She would have done what she did to get money from me one day. You only accelerated her action."

She loves me. She said she loves me just the way I am. I pull her into my arms carefully. She is mine finally. Completely. She hugs me back, and my heart warms. She pulls out of my arms and looks into my eyes, "Will you tell me now where you were going to take me this weekend before this fiasco happened?" I laugh at her question and put some of her loose strands behind her ear, "I was going to take you to Goa. So that we could relive those days we spent there."

She smiles and says, "Really? I hope we can go soon. It would have been nice to go back and spend some days there."

"You need to recover right now peacefully. Once you are completely fine to have fun, I will take you back to Goa and fuck you good till you sore your throat screaming my name, baby." I promise her. And as usual, she smirks at me.

35

Prachi- Blissful

It's been a month since I survived the kidnapping done by my former best friend. And since then, everyone has become much more protective of me. On top of those people are Ria and Arjun. They both hardly ever let me go anywhere alone. If it were up to Arjun, he would have hired bodyguards for me. I stopped talking to him after he suggested that idea. He dropped the idea after one whole day of silent treatment from me.

My parents and in-laws are extra caring now. All the attention has been getting on my nerves, but I know they all love me. Right now, I am in Jabalpur in Ria's penthouse along with Sameera and Ria. I insisted on having some girl's time, and we brought some wine. They got all kinds of

junk food. We are already drunk, and Ria has started singing songs. After a while, both Sameera and I joined her and started singing the song "South of the Border" by Ed Sheeran. I notice Sameera sings very well too. She has a soft voice. Once that song is over, I start singing "Bang Bang" by Jessie J, and again they sing with me. We continue like this for a while. We all get tired and fall to bed looking at the ceiling. We are already drunk like hell. And Sameera says,

"You guys are amazing. You both are my best friend, and I love you both"

My heart swings, and I slur, "Aww... Sam, I love you too." And Ria chimes the same. We hug each other. Sameera looks at Ria and says, "Can I ask something you, Ria? Please don't be mad at me."

Ria immediately says, "Of course, Sam. You can ask me anything. I won't get mad at you for anything."

Sameera looks at me and then again at Ria and says in a very low voice, "I saw my brother leaving your penthouse in the early morning today."

I look at Sameera and then at Ria with open mouths and start laughing. Ria looks at me, and her mouth gaps like a fish. After a while, Sameera also starts laughing, and soon Ria joins us.

After a while, Ria says, "Well, your brother is a hot piece of chocolate lava. And he spent the night with me. He sneaked out of my room this morning like a thief. Because he knew once I woke up, I would have beat his ass literally. He has been hiding from me the whole day."

Both I and Sameera are listening to her excitedly. Sameera asks the obvious question, "Since when are you both seeing each other and why haven't you told us?" She looks at me, "Did you know about this?"

Ria saves me, saying, "We do not see each other. We started as very good friends and used to hang out a lot. We ruined everything with one drunken night of sex. He insists on dating, and I keep denying it. I have been avoiding him since then. Yesterday evening we came back together in the private jet. He kept talking shit and I got drunk. He dared me into a card game. The bet was if I win he will do anything that I want and if he wins I will spend the night with him. I was so drunk I agreed to his game and I lost.

And I know he cheated in the game and tricked me because he can never beat me in a game when I am in my complete senses."

Sameera and I both look at her and start laughing our asses off. I fall out of the bed, rolling on the floor, and Sameera follows me. Ria makes a pout with her face and looks at us. Then she takes a pillow and starts hitting us with it, which makes us burst. I have tears streaming from my eyes. Finally, Sameera gets off the floor, hugs Ria, and says, "You know you can talk to me about all this right? I won't be taking anyone's side. I am like a Switzerland. But I am always here."

I hug them both, and soon we fall asleep on the bed, all over each other.

In the morning, I wake up to someone knocking on the door. Ria opens the door, and Arjun says, "If you don't mind can I take my wife? I promised her I would take her away this weekend."

Ria grunts at him from the hangover. Arjun enters the room and looks all around the room. God, we made a mess last night. Sameera is still sleeping like a baby. "How much did you guys drink last night? Are those four empty bottles of wine from last night?" Arjun asks.

I nod, and Ria goes back to sleep. Arjun picks me up in his arms, takes me to my room, and gets me a coffee while I shower. After I feel a little better from the hangover, I meet my parents and in-laws. After that, Arjun and I travel to Goa. We reach there by afternoon. We checked ourselves into the hotel.

Arjun asks the hotel service to pack some food for us while I change my clothes. I wear a purple strappy dress with violet flowers on it. Arjun smiles at me and says, "You look beautiful as always, baby. Come on, let's go. Otherwise, we will miss the sunset. We get into a car, and Arjun takes me to a secluded beach. Once again, we are alone in the whole place. Arjun drops the food pack on a rock and comes close to me. With each of his forward steps, I take one back from him. After a while, I start running away from him, and soon he catches me, and I squeal and laugh. He takes me into the water and removes my dress. I am wearing a purple bikini underneath it. He smiles at me and kisses me with so much power that it melts me into a messy puddle. I removed his t-shirt and clung to him as he took me deep into the water, kissing me the whole time. He takes us to a rock in the water, and like on our honeymoon, he pushes me onto the rock's surface. He pushes two fingers into my core, pushing my bikini bottoms aside, and starts finger fucking me while biting me below my neck. Once I come, he pushes his cock inside me in one go, and I jolt with force. "Say it, baby!" he commands.

I hold on to his neck, look into his eyes, and say, "I love you, Arjun." His breathing gets faster, "You are mine."

"Only your's," I reply while he keeps stroking inside me.

"You are my everything, Prachi."

About The Author

Pearl's Narration

I am an avid reader and addicted to books. I have been fascinated with the art of storytelling since my childhood. My parents always used to entertain me by telling stories with vivid details which got ingrained in my brain.

While I am not reading or writing, you can find me sketching or painting. I enjoy watching comedy series in my free time.

I have always wanted to become a writer and have been working as a freelance writer for many years while working in a 9-5 job. "A Stalker's Obsession" is my first book. Hopefully, you all will like it.

www.ingramcontent.com/pod-product-compliance
Lightning Source LLC
LaVergne TN
LVHW091045150826
845673LV00002B/473

* 9 7 9 8 8 9 2 3 3 0 3 0 5 *